DRENGR

DRENGR

AMANDA OLESEN

Paperback: 978-1-63767-906-7
eBook: 978-1-63767-907-4
Library of Congress Control Number: 2022908246

This is a work of fiction.

Ordering Information:

BookTrail Agency
8838 Sleepy Hollow Rd.
Kansas City, MO 64114

Printed in the United States of America

Contents

Dedicated to my loving husband, I couldn't have done this without you, to my supportive family, and my best friends.

To the people that never gave up on me and were my cheerleaders for this entire book.

And to the inspiration of Brynjolf. You know who you are. I adore having you as a friend and can't wait to spend time at events again.

Prologue
Courage

"Courage, to brave and endure difficulties, danger, pain, and even duress."

Two men stood inside a longhouse, fire crackling behind the large man in the chair.

A booming laugh echoed through the longhouse.

Stories were being exchanged between the two. A show of scars and the stories of how they got them could be heard.

Ulf was a man that towered over most; standing over six feet tall, barrel-chested, and built like a grizzly bear. Dark brown hair with strands of white covered his head that went down into a beard with beads woven into his tied-back hair and beard. A Thor's hammer, made of silver, hung around his neck outside the green tunic he wore.

He listened to his advisor, Audun, speak of everything that needed to be done for that day once they had finished with their stories, something of a morning ritual for the two since Ulf became Jarl of Wolf clan.

Blessings to couples, blessings of babies, checking in on harvests, checking stores for the feast hall, and any other happenstances that came their way.

Raven clan would be dropping by to renew their treaty of friendship with the new Jarl, Brynjar.

Bear clan was on edge with the increasing number of raids.

He sighed listening to the voice of his advisor as he ran his hand over his face. His mind already felt like it was going to be a long day.

"Audun, you're like a brother to me, but please. I already have a headache with everything you have thrown at me." Green eyes looked at the male standing in front of him.

"It's your job Ulf... You are Jarl, after all."

Ulf let out a long, drawn-out sigh, "There is that."

Ulf and Audun's voices rang out in the longhouse as they laughed.

"Alright, let's get this dealt with. What's first?"

"The blessings of the couples and the children could wait until later on this evening once Raven clan has dropped by. So, I would say that the first order of business is to check in on the harvests and storehouses."

Ulf got up and stretched, his arms going over his head as he did so. "Well, let's head around and check if anyone needs anything."

Ulf and Audun started to gather themselves up when the sound of a horn echoed outside.

"Raid?" Audun looked at Ulf.

Ulf just grinned like the cat that ate the canary. "Just like old times, dear friend."

Audun and Ulf headed out from the longhouse.

Their daughters ran up breathing heavily. "Longships... on the shore." The dark-haired one, Runa, started.

"They seem to have the banner of the boar." The redhead, Adania, finished

Ulf looked at his daughter, "Addy, protect the village, you and Runa hold the line. If they get past us. Don't let them get past you."

"We'll do our best father. May Odin protect you and may Thor give you strength."

He kissed Adania on the forehead and left with Audun in tow.

Running down the pathways of Jokolvikra; the yelling and sound of metal began to clash.

Ulf was covered head to toe in blood and viscera, man after man fell before his blade. The clash of sword and shield echoed through the village and into the mountains just beyond...

What felt like ages to Adania and Runa, the war horn finally sounded again. "It's over." Runa looked at her childhood friend.

Adania panted heavily. Blood covered her clothes. "Seems to be. Let's go find everyone." she sighed and went down toward the water where their father's battles had been going on.

A thick fog began to creep onto the shores of the village.

Adania and Runa froze upon seeing their fathers lay lifeless and covered in blood.

Adania and Runa bent down to put their father's weapons in their hands and crossed them over their chests.

"I hope you meet Odin in the halls of Valhalla," Adania said softly.

The following hours seemed to be nothing but a blur.

She was announced as the new Jarlskona and then, not long after, had to shoot a bow with a flaming arrow, alongside Runa, into a set of boats they had put out to sea that carried their father's bodies. A ritual to carry souls to Valhalla for the higher-ranking nobility.

Runa and Adania both pulled back the arrow and waited for the word 'loose' before they both let go of the string. The flaming arrows hit the boats and lit the wood as the two drifted off into the fog.

Adania sighed. Her world was now a whirlwind.

"Runa... since I am now Jarlskona and with your father being gone too... Would you be my Hersir?"

Runa smiled, "I wouldn't have it any other way Adania. I wouldn't let you have anyone else as your second." she teased.

"And we will have to deal with Raven clan ourselves it seems." Adania gave an exasperated sigh.

"You and politics don't really mix..." Runa crossed her arms over her chest, "But you are going to have to learn to deal with these things since you are going to be Jarlskona."

Adania nodded, "It's not something I'm looking forward to but it's what needs to be done..."

CHAPTER 1
INTEGRITY

"Integrity, to do what is morally and ethically right, no matter the consequences"

Adania Ulfdottir was a redhead with a fiery temper that matched her hair. She was the daughter of the head of her clan, known as a Jarl.

She wasn't an imposing person, especially in comparison to her father, only standing at five foot five, but she had an attitude, and that alone intimidated most people she came up against.

Freckles dotted her cheeks and nose under deep green eyes that hid behind long lashes.

Adania wore a black under-dress with a dark blue apron dress over it. Wolf brooches held her treasure necklaces made of amber, bone, and other pieces of jewelry.

A raven pendant hung from her neck to represent the wisdom of Odin... Gods knew she was going to need it.

Dark brown dyed leather adorned her head as a circlet, a kransen, as it was called. It had been her mother's. Her father had always been a stickler for tradition.

Her father made sure she was trained in most weapons and shields as she grew.

Her preferred weapon being a sword and shield though.

Her hand clutched her sword, her knuckles white and scarred. Scars not from training or anyone she had battled, but from a wolf; her first hunt.

Adania's thoughts went to her father's words and to her first hunt.

Swift motions, steady footing, bloodied hands, and clothes.

Not a flinch or a shake.

Firm grip, just like she had been taught.

Doubt took her mind as it came back to the training grounds.

A simple training dummy had her second-guessing herself and her footing was now loose. She could feel it and it angered her.

This is what her father taught her for as far back as she could remember.

Now here she was, an adult, thinking about her father's words while training... Or at least, trying to...

Her sword had barely left her hand since he died a few days prior.

Thinking back on it... The only time she didn't have it in her hands was when she slept, but even then, it wasn't far from her grasp.

"He's with mother now at least." She said to herself.

She was now Jarlskona of Wolf clan, but she felt alone.

Most men in her clan were afraid of her, or at least that's what she had assumed, only one had been able to beat her in hand-to-hand combat, and he didn't even want to marry her. He married her best friend, Runa.

Runa was her best advisor, much like her own father was to Adania's.

Adania put her sword back into its sheath and sighed to herself.

Looking around she took in the sight of the grounds, practice dummies in the area she was in, archery targets several feet away, weapon racks, sparring rings, and a few simple blacksmith tools to fix minor issues. All of this is encased in a large fence.

Leaving the training grounds, she noticed Runa standing against the wooden fence. "You really gave that dummy a work over." Runa stood about five foot seven with dark brown hair and blue eyes. She was well built with years of training, much like Adania.

No ax hung around her belt that evening. It was odd to see her without one as that was her preferred weapon among the ones that both of them had trained with.

The contrast between the two of them was like night and day. Runa was calculative and strategic; Adania was... less so.

Adania was always one to burst into battle and worry about things later, if at all. Even after years of training, it was something her father was never able to break her of, despite the amount of effort in trying to make her think about her actions and the consequences that followed. Though it had gotten better as she got older, she was still a fiery redhead, after all.

Adania shook her head and snickered, "It seems the only time my mind isn't racing is when I'm training or fighting… But even then, it seems to be everywhere of late."

"Maybe we need to find you a husband." Runa teased.

"I don't need a husband. Besides none of our men can beat me or you in hand-to-hand combat. If I get a husband, I want to make sure that he can protect me better than I can protect myself."

Runa shrugged, "I guess that's fair enough."

"Your husband has been the only one that could beat either of us. And he married you."

"Jealous?" Runa asked walking with Adania up toward the longhouse.

"Runa, you're my best friend. I'm happy that you're happy and I'm not jealous of that. If he ever makes you unhappy though. I won't hesitate to cut his head off."

Runa shook her head, "I have no doubt in my mind that you wouldn't, Adania."

Adania and Runa both walked into the longhouse for the feast that was about to start.

Reluctantly, Adania sat in the head chair.

This was the first feast the clan was having since her father's departure to Valhalla.

She was honored to take her father's place, but it was going to be a chore to live up to him.

Standing and holding a drinking horn that had been filled with mead, she let out a mournful howl and everyone in the mead hall soon followed.

"I, Adania Ulfdottir, take my place as your Jarlskona. I will do my best to lead you as my father had… I don't know if I can live up to his name, but I will do my best to be fair in judgment in all things that my judgment is needed. I will listen to each and every one of you if you have concerns or just need advice. This feast may be for me stepping up as your Jarlskona, but I want us to also remember the fallen… Family and friends may have left us, but tonight we drink and feast for them. May the howl of the wolf reach Valhalla, to those that are no longer here. Their legends will live on in our tales and in generations to come. Tonight, Valhalla welcomes more wolves!

"Skal!" was the word that rang out soon after.

'So far so good… Thought that speech wasn't that impressive' She thought to herself and began to eat.

The sun was setting when the feast had started and now it was well behind the horizon with the feast now over.

CHAPTER 2
HONOR

"Honor, to carry out, act, and live the values of the Viking code."

Adania walked down the pathways in the village thinking to herself. She would have to head to bed at some point but she wasn't ready to. Not sleeping well the last few nights made things nothing less than difficult.

Training? Sleep? Drink some more?

Her mind seemed to be going all over the place. Maybe she should go visit Randvi, the clan's seer. With her mind in chaos, it might help... Then again it might make it worse.

As if she had summoned the woman; she bumped into her.

"Randvi... I was just thinking about coming to see you."

"I know." She smirked, "Your mind is in turmoil since your father passed from this world, but do not fret he is with Odin in the halls of Valhalla." Her voice was soft as she spoke.

'That's a relief.' Adania thought to herself.

The dark-haired woman walked with Adania toward the shore. A couple of longboats were tied to the dock along with several smaller fishing boats.

The soft sound of the wood on the water was all that was heard before Randvi started talking again. "You worry too much little wolf. You are strong like your father and stubborn like your mother. You are destined for great things wolfling... Odin has granted me sight into your future... You will be a great leader and a great mother."

"Randvi... You know it's really creepy when you talk like that."

"That is the point, Adania. Odin grants me my sight. I am only allowed to tell you the parts that he wishes for me to tell."

"In all his wisdom, he didn't think to make things easier on those of us that live in Midgard?"

Randvi laughed then, "My dear, if it was that easy, everyone would try to seek the knowledge of the gods. Things must be obscure so that only those with his gift can speak of them..."

Adania sighed. The woman made sense. She still didn't have to like it though, "What else did you see... If you don't mind my asking."

"I don't mind you asking at all. It's a matter of *if* or *when* I am able to tell you."

"How did I know that was coming?" Adania picked up a rock and checked the weight of it before making it skip across the water.

"Because I have known you since the day you were born."

"There's that..." Adania shrugged. "I guess it's no use to ask then, is it?"

Randvi sat down on a large rock and watched the other skipping pebbles. "You are always welcome to ask, wolfling."

Adania looked at her then, hands on her hips, as she sighed. "You said I will make a great leader and great mother... I'm guessing I finally get married at some point."

Randvi nodded. "Is that all you wish to know?"

Adania shook her head. "Is he in Wolf clan? I'm guessing he isn't given that no one here can beat me... Sometimes I hate traditions..." She groaned.

"Do not let your father hear you speak such things... But no, he is not of the wolf... He is a fearsome warrior though. One that you will have trouble resisting." Randvi snickered slightly, "I have not seen the clan he is from nor do I know his name... I wish I could tell you more, but that is all I have seen."

Adania thought for a moment. "He must be beyond this land then if he is unfamiliar to you."

Randvi shifted on the rock she sat upon, listening to the water. Her dark eyes closed as she thought and meditated trying to hopefully get more insight for her new Jarlskona.

"You will have it rough being a woman. You have proven yourself to the men and women here that you are more than capable to lead and fight… Many outsiders will look down on you until you prove yourself worthy to them. Your future husband being one of them… Things will get rough this coming year, but they will get better afterward. You are a fighter. Prove that and nothing will stop you."

Adania listened to the woman and continued skipping rocks.

"I remember the day that you were born. Your parents were so happy. Ulf couldn't wait to announce you to the clan. As a child, you showed an ability to commune with the gods… I wish that we could have gotten to teach you the ways of the seer given your abilities at such a young age, but you were born a Jarl's daughter. I couldn't teach you as much as I wish I could have. Your mother had the same gift… She too was close to the gods, but trust me, Odin has plans for you child. Stay strong." Randvi wasn't going to tell the redhead what she had seen, if she did it would tear Adania to shreds. She would keep it to herself until the time came.

It was getting late and Adania knew she would have to go to bed… Or at least try to.

She had a lot to do in the morning. Mostly checking on her people, seeing what needed to be done, if anything.

Delegating was a large part of her job.

Despite only being one to delegate and make other people do the work, she always wanted to help and learn how to do things herself.

Though now she wouldn't be able to help very often given that's not in the Jarl… or rather Jarlskona… job description.

She wasn't really one to sit around and just watch or just delegate.

Talking to Randvi hadn't exactly helped much, but it didn't make things any worse, so she took it as a win.

"I must take my leave Randvi… If you need anything don't hesitate to ask."

The older woman shook her head, "I should be telling you that, Jarlskona."

Adania sighed, "Just because I'm the head of the clan now, doesn't mean you have to address me as such. Adania is fine, Randvi."

"As you wish then, wolfling."

Adania then headed to her bed. She needed a long sleep in her soft, warm furs.

Stripping out of her apron dress down to her chemise, she crawled into bed and stared at the ceiling thinking about what to do.

Closing her eyes, she relaxed and slowly drifted to sleep.

As she slept, she would dream; a dream of Odin and of a… Raid?

A raid on her village.

Buildings burning, smoke, ash, and… snow?

She looked around to see a figure of a man in leather armor, with dragon scales tooled into it, and a sword in hand. A red and black dragon emblazoned on the front of the armor stood out to her. She couldn't make out his face but his voice was unmistakable.

The command in his voice rippled across her skin. The hairs on the back of her neck stood straight up.

"Be watchful Wolf-kin." With that, he laughed causing shivers to go down her spine.

'Of course, he's got a sexy voice…' she thought to herself noticing she was in a brown under-dress, a red apron dress, and her jewelry.

"I'll be coming to take what's mine." His voice was gruff.

This wasn't a playful growl in his voice…

No…

It was a declaration of war.

He stood unmoving and unyielding.

Even though his voice had been soft when he had spoken, it still demanded attention as though he had yelled. The dominant energy he had was intoxicating.

Arrogant… *and* sexy?

What in Helheim? Adania thought to herself.

Odin appeared next to her wearing a dark cloak, donned in armor, his ravens on either shoulder with two wolves beside him growling.

Adania gripped her sword unable to speak. Any time she tried, nothing would come out.

"I'll see you soon, little wolf."

Odin looked at her and spoke. "A war is brewing. You will need to be ready, 'child of Wolf clan'. I will guide you. All you need to do is ask..."

With that, her dream faded.

CHAPTER 3
STRENGTH

"Strength, to train and shape the mind, body, and soul to be strong."

She awoke clutching her sword with sweat dripping down her face.

"What... in the... Helheim?"

Getting up, she quickly dressed and skipped breakfast to go find the seer.

"Randvi! I need to speak with you."

"Wolfling... It's barely above sunrise." Randvi replied rubbing her eyes with a yawn. "Can this wait until after I eat?"

"You can eat while I talk to you... Odin gave me a vision last night... And I don't know what to make of it."

Randvi moved aside from the door to let Adania into her home.

Adania sat down on the closest chair and sighed.

She began to tell the seer about her dream.

"This man... I never saw his face... but his voice... It demanded attention and respect without even asking for it. He seemed to tower over me and said he would be taking what was his... I'm not sure how to even *begin* to look at this. Odin has sent me foresight before but this seemed different..."

Randvi thought for a moment thinking over everything she had been told. "This may be who your future husband is. That is my first thought and the first feeling that I get, but to be in a dragon's armor... He's either quite the warrior or that arrogant. Maybe it's even a mix of both. It sounds like he is going to be quite the man for you."

Adania sighed. She was afraid that this is what that meant.

"Though if there was smoke and fire around you both along with snow... The snow could be the first snowfall of the year. Which is several months away at least. The fire and the smoke could represent the passion between the two of you... or he's going to raid this village. It's hard to tell as of right now, but these are my first impressions of it. I would have to meditate on this for a while before I could give you a solid answer, Wolfling."

Adania sat back in the chair and let out a heavy sigh. "I don't even know who he is... And I grew up around most of the Jarls of the other clans. I don't know of a Dragon."

Randvi nodded, "He may be the Jarl of a clan that just moved to our territory wanting to make a name for himself. Maybe he wants to prove something." She shrugged. "I'm not even sure myself. Give me a few days and I will see what the gods tell me."

"Thank you, Randvi... I appreciate it. I'm sorry for busting in like this, but I didn't know what to do, or who to talk to."

Randvi chuckled, as she leaned against the wall. "It's nothing, Wolfling. It's my job to aid when I am able. Even if that means that my Jarlskona wakes me from my sleep."

"Again, I apologize. I will bring you some mead from my father's personal stores if that helps."

Randvi smiled, "I won't turn down good mead."

Adania sighed and leaned forward in the chair. "I don't know how I'm going to deal with this when the time comes."

"All you can do is what the gods ask of you. Odin will guide you and give you the wisdom you need when you need it most."

"I know. I just don't always want to rely on the gods to grant me my wisdom or my strength. No offense to them. I just want to earn it on my own."

"This is why you will make a good leader, young wolf. Don't worry too much about it as of right now."

Adania nodded. "and again thank you, Randvi." she got up from the chair and headed out the door.

"Just remember there's going to be a lot of change this coming year. I hope you adapt well to it."

Adania nodded. "I'll do my best, Randvi." With that, she left the seer's home and went to the training grounds.

A lot was on her mind and she needed to relax a bit before everyone started waking up and needing her attention.

The training grounds weren't far from Runa's home.

Runa walked out hearing the clash of metal against wood.

"Adania? What in the Helheim? Why are you up so early?" She asked yawning. "You're never up this early."

Adania told her friend about the dream she had.

"Well, that seems... ominous."

"Yea, tell me about it... Also, I'm going to have to borrow your husband... I need to train and he's the only male willing to train with me."

Runa grinned and then snickered some, "At least come inside for some breakfast. You can't expect to listen to problems all day and delegate on an empty stomach."

"I can't just have you deal with it today?"

"No. *You* are Jarlskona. I am not. Besides what kind of precedence would that set for your people?"

Adania gave an aggravated sigh. "Fine." she sighed. There was really no point in arguing with Runa. Many had tried... and many of them failed.

She walked into Runa's home and it was already warm from a fire to cook breakfast. The smell of spices filled her nose along with the smell of warm bread. Honeyed meat from the night before along with fruits and vegetables were also on the fire.

"Smells so good..." Adania's mouth instantly started to water at the smell of good food.

"Granted it's not much but it's something to put in your system. And you can ask the man of the house when he wakes up." Runa grinned. "I'm normally awake before he is anyway due to making breakfast..."

"Runa, you are, as always, amazing."

"In order to be your hersir... I have to be." she teased.

Adania snickered and then sighed thinking about her father. "We both have some pretty big shoes to fill..." she trailed off.

Runa grabbed a cup and put some milk in it. "All we can do is try. Sure, we're gonna make mistakes along the way, but we need to find what works for us and for Wolf clan."

"You're right... I can't be the same way as my father 'cause we're not the same person."

Runa nodded. "All we can do is use their ways as an example and find what works for us."

Adania looked at the cup of milk in front of her and sighed again.

She felt like she still had a large weight on her shoulders that she wasn't ready to bare.

"Ladies... I thought I heard the young Jarlskona's voice grace my house."

"Ugh... Gunnar seriously. You don't have to act like that. I'm still Adania despite the title of Jarlskona."

"He's always been a flirt. I can't stop him from it. So, I just have learned to live with it."

"He's harmless... I don't take him seriously half the time anyway, Runa."

"I know... and I know you're not the only one who doesn't." Runa grinned.

"Ladies... You wound me." Gunnar put his hand on his chest as if a spear had gone through it.

"I think he's more a ham than anything..." Runa teased and gave a snicker.

Adania just rolled her eyes and put a hand to her head. "And this is what I have to put up with when it comes to my advisor couple." she teased.

"You wouldn't have us any other way," Gunnar spoke after his melodrama.

"You're not wrong." Adania smiled and ate breakfast with Runa and Gunnar explaining her dream to him and asking if he would train with her.

"I don't see a problem with it... We need a strong Jarlskona, and if you want to train with me then I don't mind."

"Plus, you're the only one that doesn't seem intimidated by my presence." Adania shrugged. "Most of the men seem to not enjoy the fact that I have kicked ass laying all of them out, aside from you."

Gunnar grinned. "That's because I'm the best you got."

Adania rolled her eyes again. "We'll start today once I get breakfast and deal with my duties... And please don't go easy on me because I'm a woman."

"Wouldn't dream of disappointing my Jarlskona."

They ate breakfast and Gunnar went outside to the training grounds with Adania.

"So, what seems to be the issue, Jarlskona?"

"Ugh... Gunnar please, just call me Adania."

"Alright... You seem to be touchier than normal, what's going on?"

She sighed, "Nothing gets passed you, does it?"

"Not normally."

Again, she sighed, hand on the hilt of the sword she wore, "With my dad now gone, I have to take over. I don't know if I'm ready for that kind of thing yet. Plus, on top of it, I keep having strange dreams that I can't make any sense of."

"Sounds like you have a loaded plate."

"That's not even the half of it... I worry that I'm not going to be a good leader for all of you, I worry that I'm not going to live up to the expectations of everyone and try to live up to my father's legacy. What if I fall short? What if everyone hates me? What if I'm doing this all for nothing?"

Gunnar shook his head. "Adania, you are strong and you know your way around a battlefield better than most of your best fighters. Don't sell yourself short. You will make a great Jarlskona. So don't try to live up to your father. You're not him. Live up to yourself. That's all you can do. As for if you are ready? Maybe not."

"Thanks for that..."

"No. No. Let me finish." He smiled at her then. "You may not feel ready and that's fine. But you have Runa and the rest of us to help where we can. Don't try to stick the entire burden on yourself."

Adania thought for a moment. "Thanks, Gunnar."

"Ready?"

"Let's go."

Gunnar and she took to the training field, sparring until they were both panting, and severely out of breath.

"Best seven out of ten." Gunnar looked at her, trying to catch his breath while holding his side.

Adania snickered as her chest heaved. "Not likely Gunnar. Thank you for this… I needed it."

Runa watched against the fence. "You ready to take on your duties now?" she scolded.

Adania grinned. "I guess so. I need to go check on everyone, see if there's anything that needs to be done, and check on people to see if they need help with anything."

Gunnar chuckled. "Would you like help, Jarlskona?"

Adania hit him in the arm playfully. "Adania… For the love of Thor, how many times do I have to tell you…" she sighed.

Runa snickered. "Come on you two. Let's get the day started and see where it goes… I know sitting in the Jarl's seat isn't anything glorious like you're looking for, but it needs to be done."

Adania sighed. "I know, I know… Thank you, Runa. This is why you are my hersir because, to be honest… I probably wouldn't get a whole lot done if you weren't." she snickered and headed toward the longhouse to start her day.

She splashed her face with water after she made the trek to the longhouse and wiped her face on her apron dress. "Alright… Well at least no one needed anything on the way here, so maybe today might be an easy day?" She looked at Runa and Gunnar with hopeful eyes.

Runa sighed. "Most likely not. Everyone is still waking and starting the day."

Gunnar stood on the opposite side of Adania as the three of them spoke and laughed.

Several hours had passed before there was a dispute that needed to be dealt with.

Sighing she listened to the two males argue back and forth for what felt like a lifetime. "Alright, I've had enough. Since neither of you can come to an agreement and since no matter what I or Runa suggest that you do, neither of you wishes to do that. So, we're going to settle this the old-fashioned way. A Holmgang to first blood. I don't want any more deaths in Wolf clan right now. So, first blood and let that be the end of it. Got it?" She growled as a headache started. "Is this sufficient? Or do I have to beat both your faces in myself and send you to opposite corners of the village?"

"It's fine by me." The dark-haired male hung his head.

"As by me." The blonde man spoke softly then.

Adania sighed, "alright, make a square out in the back of the longhouse."

Runa and Gunnar nodded and headed out of the doors to begin making the square for the Holmgang as Adania looked at the two males. "After this, I expect someone to owe another an apology and you two make up. You both are too valuable to this clan for the two of you to be on the outs. You're both fine artisans and tradesmen."

"Yes, Jarlskona." The blonde sighed looking at the ground.

"Trygve... It'll be fine. You are one of our best craftsmen. No one comes close to your brooches. Same with Olan and his weapon making. Honestly, I think both of you could learn things from one another if you both weren't so stubborn." she walked them both outside toward the ring that Runa and Gunnar had made.

"Just remember first blood. I'm not giving either of you weapons because I don't want either of you to have a severe injury and then we have to take you to Randvi... Fists and feet only. Got it?"

The blonde, Trygve, nodded. "Yes Jarlskona."

She looked at Olan, the dark-haired male, and he nodded in agreement.

"First blood and I expect a fair fight or you're going to be in major trouble."

"Of course, Jarlskona.." Both males agreed and headed to the roped-off area that only housed about twelve feet square.

Once everything was set, Adania sighed.

The holmgang began and went on for several minutes.

After what felt like an eternity with Adania and Runa watching intently, Trygve landed the blow to draw first blood.

Olan spat blood upon the ground. "Nice one Trygve." He grinned. "I yield."

Adania grinned and folded her arms across her chest. "Now that that is settled. No more arguing over this matter, but I will ask that you both take a lesson from one another once in a while on how things are done within your craft. That way both of you will understand a little bit more and maybe never have this argument again. But in true old fashion of this holmgang it is now done and I trust that both of you will uphold the honor of it. No more arguing. Let this issue be buried and dealt with. The gods have chosen. Now let's head back to the longhouse so that I may deal with more of my Jarl duties." she groaned.

Runa snickered, "You're just like your father."

Adania looked at Runa in disbelief, "I beg to differ."

Gunnar shook his head, "and the two of you are much like your fathers. Dear Jarlskona, you hate the boring aspects of court and law much like your own father. You would rather be on the battlefield with a sword and shield in your hand, and my dearest Runa is constantly having to play escort to make sure that you do in fact do those Jarl duties that you are not so fond of."

Now that it was spoken aloud, Adania couldn't argue about it. She did in fact hate sitting in the Jarl's chair. Well, not hate it... but she sure didn't enjoy it.

She shrugged... It was all she could do. Going back up to the longhouse she finished the day without issue.

Standing up from the wooden chair she stretched and felt her back pop. "That felt nice..." she sighed and looked to Runa and Gunnar. Runa just shook her head. "What?"

"You sound like an old woman."

"You sit up on that chair all day without something to sit on."

"Please forgive me Jarlskona for not finding something for your delicate rear end. I will be sure to bring one for you on the 'morrow." Runa spoke sarcastically with a grin.

Adania sighed and put her hands on her hips, cocking them to the side. "Seriously Runa? Must we do this?"

Runa snickered and looked at her childhood friend. "At least until you find a husband who can annoy you as much as I do."

"Once I find a husband then he can sit in that chair and deal with talking to people..." Sighing again she rubbed her backside now that she was gaining feeling back in. Something she hadn't noticed until now. "I swear that chair conformed to my father's backside with how long he sat there. I'm surprised there's not divots in the wood shaped like his ass." she groaned.

Runa rolled her eyes. "Well, then we will just have to ask our dear Astrid to make you a new seat for your delicate ass to sit in."

Adania pouted, "Runa… Why are you always so mean to me?"

Runa shook her head again, "Because you need someone to keep you in line."

Adania just snickered then, "Well, you're not wrong." she shrugged. "But I need to head home and eat… Then I might train some more. I don't know yet. It all depends on what I decide to eat and what I might snack on before bed."

"It better not be anything that will make you puke up your insides."

Adania shook her head, "As much as I enjoy mead and ale… It's not something that I will drink heavily on." With that Adania went to go find herself something to eat for dinner.

Chicken? Cow? Pig? Lamb?

'Should I go out hunting and find something that way?' She thought to herself.

If that were the case, she would have to ask Runa or someone to go with her, and Runa would most likely scold her the entire time and scare away any hope of a rabbit or venison.

Sighing to herself she decided she would just make a steak and some parsnips. Raspberries would be her snack before bed.

Smiling to herself she made her food and then ate as she thought back upon her day.

Gods did she have some large shoes to fill. Her father was most likely looking down on her and scolding her from his seat in Valhalla.

Once she was finished, she cleaned up her mess and sighed again.

The whirlwind of the last few days finally started to settle down.

Going to bed she curled up against her pillows and her furs.

That night she was quick to fall asleep, which was a blessing considering the previous nights.

CHAPTER 4
EMPATHY

"To see things from more than one perspective before passing judgment."

She awoke the next morning from a dream much like before.

The man in leather with a voice that demanded attention and the way it crawled across her skin made her want to melt back into the furs to sleep in order to hear him again.

"The dragon..." she whispered to herself. Sighing, she got up and dressed.

She would have to focus on her dream later.

Adania hadn't even heard Runa walk in.

Although, Runa almost landed flat on the floor because of the hug from behind she had given the redhead.

"Odin's beard... You scared the shit out of me Runa."

Runa laughed. "I'm surprised you're even up this early. You always did enjoy sleeping in. I thought I would check on you and see if I could make you breakfast."

Adania sighed. "Alright, I know better than to argue with you."

"Also... I wanted to tell you. My bleed is late. So... I may be having a baby."

Adania smiled. "Runa. That's wonderful. I hope that the baby is healthy and acts just like you." she teased.

Runa rolled her eyes. "Don't curse me with a child that's just like myself."

Adania laughed then. "Serves you right for all the shit you've given me."

Both women spoke of the day and Adania mentioned the dream she had. The same one with the man dressed in leather.

Both came up empty on what the dream could mean, though Adania was starting to get an inkling as to what it meant. She didn't want to admit that that was what it meant, however.

Ignoring it, for now, was her best option.

After eating the first meal of the day she went outside; noticing two ravens sitting on the fencing that surrounded the area.

"Odin... please do not tell me that you are sending me a husband... I can't handle it right now."

A soft breeze hit her face.

'Fenrir, Lord of wolves, give me the strength to deal with this and the speed to do so quickly.' Adania prayed to herself. Sighing, she went about her work around the longhouse.

A few weeks had passed. She was outside the longhouse hearing the war horns.

"For the love of Thor..." she groaned.

Yet another raid.

Raids had been happening a *lot* recently.

She couldn't even call on Raven clan or some of the other allies as they too were being raided by banners unknown to her.

'Was this the work of the dragon?' She thought to herself.

"Runa, longhouse."

"I can fight."

"Not when you're with child and if we lost you and the baby, Gunnar would never forgive me. You're one of my best. Protect the children. If Gunnar, my other warriors, and myself can do our jobs correctly then you won't have to worry much."

"Adania..."

"We'll be fine." She assured her friend.

"You better be."

With that Adania left to meet the ones that held the serpent's banner.

"Gunnar... with me."

"Naturally. Someone has to protect your backside when Runa isn't around."

"Always the flirt. You do know I'm not interested."

"I know, but that doesn't mean it's not fun to see the look on your face when I do it."

She snickered. "I definitely could use a laugh right now."

"We have our best warriors on it, so it will be fine."

Adania smiled. "That we do... Aside from your wife, I'm not letting her pregnant ass anywhere near this."

"I would have fought her too if she didn't listen to you, so there's that."

Adania grinned. Sword and shield in hand.

Upon reaching the center of Jokolvikra she let out a loud howl. Everyone around her followed suit and it soon echoed throughout the village.

It wasn't long after that the clash of sword and shield began. Yelling filled the village and went well into the mountains behind it.

Adania was covered in blood and viscera. Blood that she wore like war paint.

She and Gunnar fought together without having to speak much at all. They had done so much training in the last few weeks that it was almost like they could read each other's movements.

A sword came clashing down onto Adania's shield making her stagger backward into Gunnar.

"Shit..."

"You okay?"

"No worse for wear yet."

Fighting and making their way toward the longboats that had hit their shores, more blood and viscera decorated the thoroughfares.

Seeing the archers on the longboats drawback, Adania yelled, "Shields!"

Everyone around her as well as herself raised their shields to catch the flying arrows that came their way.

Dropping her shield, she took off running toward the longboats; losing sight of Gunnar and a few of her other warriors in the process of doing so.

Without the shield, she was able to move around a lot better. She much preferred fighting with only a sword. It allowed her a better range of movement.

The love of battle made her forget the stress of her position as Jarlskona of her clan.

Her heart raced and her body moved without a second thought as she fought the archers on the longboat.

Once the last archer of the invading forces fell, she heard a condescending clapping. Looking around she noticed she did have a few of her clan mates around her on the ship, but Gunnar was nowhere to be found.

The man that was clapping wasn't a large man and she felt she could easily take him.

He wasn't much taller than she was. This wasn't the man from her dreams.

This man just seemed like a pompous windbag with no ability to back it up. After all, he wasn't even fighting with his warriors on the ground. He stayed on the longboat as if that would have saved him.

Adania was fuming. This man was a coward. "Take your ships and leave."

"Or what little wolf? Many know your father has departed to Odin's halls and many want this village as their own. The trade that comes in and out of here, the ore and stones you get from your mountains. Everyone wants a piece of it."

"Over my dead body. I am more than willing to trade and treaty with clans. These raids are really starting to piss me off." She glared at the man then and still didn't drop her stance. "You are a coward. I don't trade with spineless curs."

"Oh, the little wolfling has some bite to her."

"You stayed on your ship in hopes that we wouldn't make it this far passed your warriors. Just so you know… They can't fight worth shit."

His eyes flared in anger.

'Oh, I hit a nerve.' she thought to herself and gave a wolf-like grin.

Adania stood tall but still not dropping her guard. "Leave Wolf clan lands or I will spill your blood upon your boat and send the survivors back to your homelands. Unless of course, they wish to join Wolf clan.

They would be led by someone who would actually fight alongside them... It seems that you want all the glory with none of the fight for it. Odin wouldn't want such a whelp within his halls... Now you can turn your ships and leave or I send you to Niflheim myself."

"If you think you can little wolf."

"I hope I send you to Nastrond so that Nidhogg may feast upon your corpse."

"If you weren't so mouthy you would make a pretty wife."

"You couldn't handle a wolf woman, let alone a subservient one... So again, you can either leave or I send you to the Shores of Corpses."

"I'm not leaving. I'm taking what's mine."

Adania laughed and readied her blade. "Fine by me... Though none of this is yours to take."

With that, he lunged at her wildly.

His anger and rage blinded him in the battle, while she remained calm and fluid.

Within minutes his head separated from his body. Turning to the ones that still survived she looked at them. "If you want to go back to your homelands, I will allow it. Gather your dead or leave them here if you wish. I will give you seven days."

A man spoke up then. "You are the sitting head of Wolf clan?"

"Yes... Adania Ulfdottir is my name."

"Adania... I am Ivar Bjornson. I will be the one that will be in charge from now on."

Adania nodded in acknowledgment, "As long as you don't try to kill me, you are welcome in these halls. If you wish to make a treaty or trade agreement then I will be happy to discuss such things."

"I would have to go back to my Jarl and speak with him on such a matter, but I appreciate the idea. I don't know if any of us will join Wolf clan as we are quite happy in our homelands. None of us wished to come here and wake the wrath of the wolf." He chuckled.

"You are not the first raiders to come here. I just wish that I had more warriors to fight."

"If any of my kinsmen wish to join you, I will not stop them. You fight well, Adania."

"Thank you."

"You were trained well. But I will allow you to give rites to those that have fallen since this is your land."

"You and your kinsmen are more than welcome to stay here until the burial rites are carried out."

"Then we shall help with such things. I'm sure those born to Fenrir do a few things differently than those of us born of Jormungandr."

She snickered slightly. "I mean no disrespect with my snicker. I am just thinking on the situation. Your raid party leader's attitude was vastly different than yours is."

He too snickered then. "Granted, I am no coward when it comes to fighting, but again none of us wanted to be here to begin with. He insisted that he could beat the new head of Wolf clan and tame her as his."

She snorted as she laughed. "Forgive me…"

"Nothing needs to be forgiven… He was an ass. I told him that once we got here I wasn't going to help him fight any of you. I just want to go back home and tend my duties."

Adania walked off the longboat with Ivar and spoke with him about the following few days and the rites of the dead.

Chapter 5

Hospitality

"Everyone should be treated with dignity and courtesy."

Adania walked through Jokolvikra wrapped in her cloak a few days after the raid.

Gunnar was among the fallen and she felt absolutely horrible about it. She hadn't been able to protect him like she had promised Runa.

Runa, of course, wasn't mad about it. "He's a warrior and he is within Odin's halls. He was protecting you and me as well as the clan. He was honorable. I'm sad that I lost him but this is Odin's will."

Adania hugged her friend tightly. "Still though..."

Runa shook her head. "No but still. This is what he wanted. He always said he wanted to go out in a blaze of glory so that Odin knew he was coming."

Adania and Runa snickered some. "If you need anything, let me know."

"You needn't worry Adania, if I need anything then you will be the first to know..."

Ivar walked up into the longhouse then. "Adania, we have finished preparations for the rites and pyres. Your presence is requested as is mine."

"Thank you, Ivar. I will be there momentarily."

The short-haired male turned and headed back the way he came. "I will let everyone know." With that, he was no longer in the longhouse.

Runa snickered. "If I didn't know you were meant for Dragon clan I would say go after him."

Adania rolled her eyes. "No. He's not my type Runa... He's so... plain."

Runa laughed and got up grabbing her drinking horn. "Let's go take care of the rites and pyres."

The red-headed woman nodded and walked with her friend down the pathways to where the pyres had been made.

She stood next to Ivar with Runa on the other side of her. Adania and Ivar were handed torches to light the pyres. Runa was given a bow with a flaming arrow.

Runa pulled back on the bowstring and let it go once Gunnar's boat was a distance away in the water. Watching it burn, she sighed to herself.

Once the pyres had been lit, Adania sighed and turned to Ivar. "I look forward to having you as some of our tradesmen."

"I look forward to us forming a good friendship in the process. I have sent letters ahead of our departure to my Jarl and I explained what happened with Orm and the fallen. I will be leading on the way back home. Some of my kinsmen wish to stay. They seem to like it here far more than home."

"Then I will welcome them as if they were always my clan and kin."

"I appreciate all that you have done for us the last few days."

Adania shook her head. "You are on my lands so it is my pleasure to take care of you."

Ivar smiled. "You have been a great host... I have heard of the hospitality of Wolf clan but hadn't actually experienced it before... I look forward to being here again."

"And I look forward to having you and your kinsmen the next time you stop on Wolf clan shores."

"We will be leaving within the next day or two."

"Take all the time you like Ivar. I can give you supplies should you need them."

He just shook his head. "You have given us more than enough."

"Well, you are always welcome here Ivar."

"Thank you, Jarlskona of Wolf clan."

"Adania is fine."

And just like that, within a few days, Ivar left with a few supplies that Adania insisted he take with him on a single ship aside from being filled with those that were heading back to Serpent clan's territory.

"Take these as an incentive to your Jarl. Do not open them until you return home." Adania instructed.

"Alright. Fine. Since you insist." He snickered.

She handed him a large wooden box filled with gems, ores, and some of their artisan's crafts.

"I'm sure he will appreciate the gift."

"A sign of good faith to trade with us. I have no hard feelings from the raid by any means. It wasn't your fault… I'm just glad that we possibly have an ally out of it."

He nodded. "Well, I look forward to seeing you more often. I am quite sure that my Jarl will want to have an ally and someone to trade ores with."

She smiled and nodded. "Have a safe journey back home. And again, you and Serpent clan are always welcome here Ivar."

"Thank you, Adania."

With that, the ship loaded up and left the shores of Jokolvikra.

She made sure that the new clansmen had homes made where there was space and made sure to get them situated.

With the number of people the clan had, it wouldn't be an issue to build a couple of houses.

In the meantime, the once Serpent clan members would stay in the longhouse with Adania or with those that offered if they had extra rooms.

Through the course of several days, a couple houses had been built and the new clan members found artisans to work with or found somewhere else to fit that suited them.

Adania sighed to herself as everything was starting to run smoothly over the next few days.

No raids… no conflicts… She wished most of her duties were this easy.

"Runa, do you think that my father would be proud of me?"

"You're not doing anything to embarrass him. So, I would say so."

Adania sighed and pulled her hair over her shoulder to play with as she sat in the Jarl's chair within the longhouse.

"But no seriously Adania, you're doing great. You've been handling these raids like you have been head of Wolf clan for years. You lead and we all follow. You're not a coward. You're right up there with the rest of us when we fight. You should have more confidence in yourself. The clan is doing well considering. Most people thought you to be weak and you have proved them wrong. Maybe things will slow down now and we can begin rebuilding everything we need to."

"I hope you're right Runa." Adania sighed and thought about the lessons from her father while she would train relentlessly... She still trained relentlessly.

"I'm not looking forward to the day I have to fight the dragon..." Adania spoke after several moments of silence.

Runa put her embroidery on her lap. "I'm sure it will be fine. If he's anything like how you have described him then I'm sure it will be fine."

Adania shrugged, "I don't know on that one... The man has an air about him that I haven't ever experienced before. I can't even begin to describe it... Let alone him."

Runa snickered, "You still haven't seen what he looks like have you?"

Adania shook her head, "Nope... Not a damned thing... He's tall... That's all I know."

Runa went back to her embroidery while she listened to her friend, "Well, that's more than you had before."

"Not really. Even far away the man seems tall and imposing."

Runa sighed, "I think you're worrying too much about it..."

Adania shrugged, "Most likely. I do overthink things... A lot."

Adania received a letter from Ivar a few days afterward about him and his Jarl coming to visit and work out trade agreements.

"Looks like Ivar made it back home and barely made his home soil and wants to travel back with his Jarl to trade with us. I guess that crate of everything we sent back with him was sufficient enough for his Jarl." Adania spoke to Runa as she read the letter.

"That's a good sign then. Maybe we will have an ally or at least a trade route adding to the ones we already trade with."

"Raven clan has always been an ally with us for as far back as I have known. Though I probably should send word to have them come here and I speak with their Jarl. My father was the last one to speak with them and we were just whelps back then. They probably don't even know that he is passed into Valhalla now." Adania shrugged. "And I wonder if I should speak with Bear's Jarl." She thought for a moment.

Runa shrugged then herself. "It wouldn't hurt any. Plus, I know they have been on edge since all the raids have been happening almost non-stop."

"The raids worry me too... We're already having issues keeping up with the warriors we do have. I don't even know if we could handle another raid, to be honest. We're stretched pretty thin..." Adania sighed. Getting up she looked at the maps of the nearby clans and which ones were closest.

"We will have to make several trips or have them come here. Our closest is Raven clan just beyond the mountains, followed by Bear, then Serpent, though I don't know about where Dragon hails. There are many lands beyond ours and most of which I don't even know. I also need to speak with the Stag, Boar, Horse, and Squirrel clans... At least those are the closest ones that I can speak with. I'm sure there are many more... But those are the ones I am familiar with that are around here and those that my father had dealings with."

"Looks like there's going to be a lot of travel in our future." Runa ran her fingers over the map.

"*My* future. You can't travel when you're pregnant... besides who would stay and defend Wolf clan."

Runa let out a groan. "I'm pregnant not an invalid."

"Not risking it."

"By the gods, you are so finicky with this. Gunnar wouldn't have acted this way."

"And I don't want him coming down from Valhalla and kicking my ass because you ended up getting hurt or something worse."

All Runa did was give an exasperated sigh. "I hate you so much."

"No, you don't. You love me to pieces." Adania smirked and poked her friend on the cheek.

Runa shook her head, "Fine. I'll stay here."

"Good... Though I might just send for them and explain that I can't travel and leave Wolf clan unprotected considering."

"I can protect Wolf clan just fine Adania."

"I never said you can't. You just shouldn't have to do it alone."

"Alright... That's fair."

Adania looked up from her maps, turned, and then leaned against the table folding her arms across her chest with her backside against the wood of the table. "But first we will meet with the Serpent clan Jarl in a few days and then we will go from there. I have a feeling that things are about to get… chaotic."

"You know what happens when you say that. Loki always rears his head going, *'You asked for me?'*" Runa looked at Adania with concern.

"I just hope that I am prepared for what he has in store for me."

"I wouldn't worry about it until the time comes."

"I guess so, but it still worries me either way."

A few more days had passed and Adania and Runa met the longboat of Serpent clan at the docks.

Greeting the Jarl and Ivar she smiled. "It is good to see you again Ivar."

"Likewise, Jarlskona. This is my Jarl…"

A man standing slightly taller than Adania, with an athletic build, walked off the longboat after speaking with a few of the longboat crew. He wore a red and blue tunic with embroidery of serpents weaving in and out of one another around the collar. His head was shaved on either side with the hair on the top of his skull pulled back with tattoos on either side of his head close to his ears. Symbols of Jormungandr decorated the left side of his head while the right had runes of strength, protection, and victory.

"Welcome to Jokolvikra."

"I am Jerrick Sigurdson. Jarl of Serpent clan. I heard that you were quite something on the battlefield and I wanted to thank you for the gifts that you so graciously sent." He held out his hand.

Adania took his wrist and pulled him into a sideways hug with a firm smack to his shoulder blade. "It wasn't a problem Jerrick. I figured I would send you samples of what we can offer as trade with you. I would much rather have an ally than an enemy."

Jerrick let out a snicker, making his blue eyes shimmer, as they began walking up toward the longhouse. "Enemies are a part of life young wolfling."

"I know that but I need to make allies just the same and prove to everyone that I can be a great Jarlskona just as my father was a great Jarl."

"I drank a horn for your father once I found out that he had passed to Valhalla."

"Thank you." Adania showed the two around Jokolvikra before going to the longhouse.

"But I am sure that you will do him proud as the head of Wolf clan. You have already proven to be an apt warrior. Even Ivar was impressed and the man doesn't impress easily."

"Well then. I'm glad I could stand up and impress him then."

"It's one reason that we are happy to have a trade route with Wolf clan. You are a strong woman, Adania. Don't sell yourself short."

"Thank you, Jerrick. It means a lot to hear it from someone outside my clan. Runa tells me that I am doing a good job and that I'm doing my father proud but I can't help but think she's biased." she snickered. "I have known her since we were barely walking."

Jerrick laughed, "I have known Ivar about as long so I know what you mean."

The four of them walked into the longhouse and sat down at a table.

Discussing the trades and exchanges took a few hours.

"You are more than welcome to stay for a few days if you like, you can meet some of the artisans or you can head back. It's entirely up to you. I know your journey is a few days from here at least... I would like you all well rested before you leave."

"I think we shall stay for a few days... If you don't get tired of us by then."

Adania snickered. "Not at all. As long as you behave yourselves and don't cause problems then you are welcome to stay as long as you like."

"Alright then. We shall stay a few days and then head back to Serpent territory."

"I can provide clothes if you need them and I have a couple of extra beds here in the longhouse if you wish to stay here."

"I have plenty of clothes as does Ivar. Ivar and I will stay here in the longhouse the rest of the longboat crew will most likely stay with the kinsmen that have joined with you."

"That is quite fine. I can show you around more in the next few days and show you more of what the Wolf craftsmen can do. I look forward to the friendship, Jerrick."

"As do I, Adania." Jerrick and Ivar stood up and bowed slightly. "I will dismiss myself and go fetch my things."

Ivar nodded. "More like I will be fetching his things..."

Adania snickered. "I will show you both to your rooms once you return. And if you would like a bath, I can show you to the pond that we use."

"That sounds wonderful Adania, thank you."

Both men went back to the docks, while Adania and Runa got a couple of the rooms ready in the longhouse.

Ivar and Jerrick returned sometime later with a couple of bags each.

"You don't seem to have much," Adania commented.

Runa looked up and nodded in agreement. "Adania always takes so much with her when she travels." she snickered.

Adania sighed. "I guess it's just a girl thing."

Jerrick and Ivar laughed. "Well, we pack light when we're only going to be gone for a few days."

"Now about that bath." Ivar looked at the two women.

Adania smiled. "Of course." She snickered. "It's not far from the longhouse actually. I can show you the way... Runa go ahead and head home. I think I can handle the rest of the night."

"You sure? Cause if these two do anything untoward with you. I will murder them."

"Runa. They are our guests. I'm sure they will behave themselves."

Jerrick snickered. "She's like a sister."

Adania sighed. "Yes, she is. She's older than I am by several months... She's also going to be having a baby... I'm sure the motherly instincts are kicking in."

Runa put her hands on her hips and huffed slightly. "They better behave themselves."

"For the love of Thor, Runa! Go to bed. Gods you're so cranky." Adania gave an exasperated sigh. "I can handle myself. Now go rest."

Runa sighed and soon left the longhouse to go back to her own home.

CHAPTER 6

BROTHERHOOD

"To nurture friendships with others for this life and the next"

Adania lay in bed that night thinking about all the lessons her father had taught her.

Closing her eyes, she sighed and drifted off to sleep.

Her dream showed her as a little girl sitting in her father's lap as he sat on one of the chairs. She was playing with a small wooden wolf that Ulf had carved for her.

They were sitting at the first Althing that she could remember attending.

The Althing, a grand assembly to exercise legislative power, or something like that. Her father had explained earlier that day what was going on, but she was more interested in playing with Runa and her toys than learning about the duties she would eventually have to take the mantle for.

Audun had come with them being Ulf's second in command, leaving the fighters and Adania's mother to defend Wolf clan.

Adania wasn't really paying attention to the politics of the Althing until there was almost a fight break out.

Luckily Ulf stopped it before it got too out of hand. He sat Adania down on his seat. Audun and Runa were seated beside her.

Adania strained to watch the carnage hoping to see a fist fight or swords get drawn.

Runa sighed, "we're at the Althing Addy... You're not going to see much here. It's all politics."

Adania groaned, "Oh come on I wanna see some blood. This is boring..."

"You're going to have to learn to deal with these things eventually."

"Can't I learn about this kind of stuff later?"

Runa smacked Adania in the back of the head, "If you learn about it now then it will be easier when you get older."

Adania rubbed the back of her skull. "Gods... Why are you so mean?"

"Someone has to keep you in line."

"You are barely one winter older than I. That's not even fair."

Audun chuckled at the two. "Calm down you two and watch. You will get to see as too why your father is Jarl of the Wolf clan." He whispered.

Adania stood up on the chair in order to have a better view.

Ulf sighed and walked over to the two arguing and separated them. "Gentles... How about we settle this with a game of flyting? Entertain the crowd whilst we wait for the Althing to begin again?"

"A flyting?" Adania looked up at Audun.

Audun nodded. "Aside from the Holmgang... sometimes we settle things with a game of flyting. It's a game of wit and intellect. Granted there is no bloodshed but it's a way to show you have a lethal tongue and quick wit."

"Oh... That's boring." Adania pouted.

Audun just laughed. "Your father was pretty good at it at one time."

"Dad was boring?" She cocked her head to the side and looked back at the crowd.

Audun sighed. "Just watch Adania. I promise it is far less boring than it sounds."

Ulf stood between the two males watching.

The younger of the two smirked. "Age before beauty."

"I see you have done this before."

"I have. Many a time."

"Alright then... let's see here..." The older man thought for a moment. "You sir, are repugnant and absurd."

The younger male acted as though he had been wounded and then readjusted himself to standing straight. "Good sir. I beg your pardon. I shall remain unvexed and unstirred."

The younger male crossed his arms over his chest then; ready to start the next round.

Ulf gave a nod to begin.

"That tunic is garish and appalling." The younger man made himself visibly shudder for effect.

The older man seemed unphased and shook his head. "I hear you can't hold your ale. You're always on the floor sprawling."

Adania watched the back and forth between the two. "This is... flyting?"

Audun nodded. "Yes. One person insults another, of course in good fun, and the other person has to make a rhyme to the previous person's insult."

"Huh... You have to be really good with words then."

"That you do, little wolfling."

The older man looked at Ulf who gave a nod. "Stealing your mother's clothes. That's really quite rude."

"Are you old and senile? Your vision seems skewed."

Ulf laughed some, "Alright, alright. It is done... Let's see who won this one... The mighty old boar?" There was some cheering for the older man. "Or the young dragon?" Many more cheers were heard for the younger male.

"Excellent show... Though it seems the young dragon has taken this win. I shall get you a drink later this evening."

"That was much fun. I haven't had a time like that in a while."

"I am Ulf by the way. Jarl of Wolf clan." He held his hand out and the younger male graciously took it.

"Pleasure is mine Ulf. I am Hrani of Dragon clan. I'm sure my son is around here somewhere."

Ulf nodded, "I have my daughter with me. She wasn't going to take no for an answer on staying with her mother."

"Is she a redhead?"

"Most definitely. Just like her mother."

The two shared a laugh then.

Hrani whistled and a small boy came running up. His dark brown hair was tied back. "Yes, father?"

"This is Ulf of Wolf clan. He brought his daughter here. Maybe you two can play together so that you won't be bored while we deal with the Althing."

"I don't want to play with a girl." The boy pouted.

"Brynjolf…"

Ulf laughed some and bent down to be eye-level with the boy. "Well. My little Addy isn't like other girls. She loves to fight and roughhouse and enjoys giving people bloody noses."

"No girl likes that stuff."

Ulf snickered and motioned for Audun to bring the girls over.

Adania hopped off Ulf's chair and went running across the floor over to her father seeing him motion for them.

Headbutting him in the hip she snickered.

Ulf groaned slightly. "Addy. Right on time." He sighed and tried to straighten himself up.

The boy stood looking skeptically at the red-headed girl.

"What're you looking at?"

Brynjolf snickered, "I'm looking at what I think is supposed to be a lady."

"At least I'm old enough to not look like a baby," Adania smirked making her green eyes glitter from the firelight.

Ulf looked down at Adania. "You see flyting one time and now you think you can flyt yourself?"

Adania shrugged. "I learn fast father. You know this."

Hrani laughed, "You're going to have your hands full with that one Ulf."

"She is my only. This is Adania…" He patted her head and looked back at Hrani as they began talking.

Audun and Runa came up not long after. "What did we miss?"

"Not a whole lot. Hrani is from Dragon clan and brought his boy. I thought the kids could go play together so they wouldn't be bored here listening to us old men talk about boring things."

Audun nodded, "Well, Runa seems to want to be involved in the Althing and wants to learn about it. So if she wants to stay or go that's up to her. Though she might fall asleep once everything gets underway again."

Ulf nodded. "All three can go play in the snow. Let them be kids after all. They don't have to be involved in this until they're much older."

Adania stood by Runa and then pulled her and the boy out of the large longhouse and shoved them both in the snow laughing.

The three ended up throwing snowballs at each other until their fingers went numb.

Laughing they went back inside to warm up by one of the fires while the meeting continued.

Looking around Adania noticed bread on one of the tables. Grinning she looked at Runa and Brynjolf. "I'm gonna get us that bread." She whispered.

"Adania." Runa scolded.

"What? I'm hungry and I'm sure you are too."

Before Runa could say anything Adania slinked away. Going to the table she grabbed one of the small loaves of bread and brought it back. Ripping it into three pieces she handed the two their pieces and devoured hers.

Going back to the table she asked one of the serving maids if she could get a couple cups of water for her and her friends.

The woman nodded and smiled. Bringing the cups of water, she handed Adania one and walked with her over to the other two, handing them their own cups.

"Thank you." Adania smiled and watched the fire crackle slightly.

"You're welcome." The woman bowed and then left to continue with her other duties.

"You two are definitely not like the girls from my clan," Brynjolf spoke softly.

"Oh? How so?"

"Most of them are way too ladylike and don't want to get dirty... While the bottoms of your dresses are coated in mud."

"And? We're Wolf clan. We're taught to be ladies, yes, but that doesn't mean we act like it all the time."

Runa sighed and shook her head. "You almost never act like a lady Adania."

Adania stuck her tongue out at Runa. "At least we can fight, unlike most girls we've met from other clans. And I'm pretty sure I scared all the boys of Wolf clan anyway..." She shrugged.

Adania heard her father talking about what it meant to be Wolf clan.

Courage, honor, strength, brotherhood, loyalty, integrity, discipline, determination...

She could hear him speak to others about treaties and trades.

"I guess the Althing is all about trade agreements and whatnot." Adania sighed and looked at the other two.

Runa sighed, "I'm sure there's more to it than that."

Adania shrugged, "That's what it sounds like dad is talking about."

Adania awoke rubbing her head from a headache. "Odin... What are you trying to tell me?" she asked herself and sighed.

Getting up she dressed and waited for Ivar and Jerrick while she ate breakfast trying to remember the dream she had.

It wasn't like her to not remember them.

Runa walked into the longhouse as Adania was eating some sweet bread. "You're up early."

"Had a dream last night..."

"And?"

"I can't remember it."

Runa looked at her and blinked a few times. "I hope it wasn't important."

"I remember it being about us and the first time we went to the Althing as kids but that's all I remember."

"Ah... I vaguely remember that myself."

Adania gave a frustrated sigh, "I really hope this isn't some prank from Loki, especially if it's important."

Runa nodded. "I'm sure it's nothing Adania. Also, we have the harvest festival coming up, and we need to start planning for that."

Adania gave another frustrated sigh, as she brought her fingers to the top of her nose to pinch it, hoping the headache would go away.

"Adania, are you alright?"

"I just had a dream that I can't remember, and I woke up with a headache. It's nothing."

Runa sighed and shook her head. "I know by now not to question you if you say it's nothing, but you should take it easy today. Maybe you're just worrying yourself too much, or working too much."

Adania shook her head. "I'll be fine."

Runa let out a sigh of frustration herself then. "Alright, but if you need to rest, then I want you to tell me so I can handle the day for you."

"Thank you, Runa, but I'm sure it's nothing… Maybe I should go see Randvi and see what she says. I can talk to her later and see what she says, but it's probably not going to be much honestly." She shrugged.

"Probably just give me a salve or some mixture to help with my head."

"It's better than nothing." Runa sighed. "But if that's what you want then I won't push you."

Ivar and Jerrick walked into the longhouse then and laughed as they were talking to one another.

"Morning." Adania smiled and stood up to greet them.

"Morning Adania. What are the goings on today?" Jerrick asked as he sat down with Ivar, Adania, and Runa.

"Well, Runa and I do have some festival planning today. Granted it's not for another month or so but planning it now makes it easier to deal with later. However, you are more than welcome to walk around Jokolvikra all you like, or join us and see how we plan things."

Jerrick shrugged. "I don't mind tagging along for some festival planning."

Ivar nodded. "I always enjoy a good festival, especially when mead is involved."

Adania snickered, "Well, we have a mead that we make with juniper, cloudberries, and lingonberries."

Ivar grinned, "That sounds absolutely delicious."

Jerrick hit his chest, "Ivar… Behave."

Adania and Runa snickered again, "It's fine Jerrick. The way we make Wolf mead is pretty famous on its own."

Ivar looked at Jerrick, "See… She said it was fine."

Jerrick rolled his eyes, "She is being a gracious host…"

Adania looked at both of them, "I can send you home with some. We have been working on some of it for a while now. We normally make it and let it sit for a year and then we drink it at the harvest festival."

Jerrick smiled and nodded, "Sounds good to me. I'm sure Ivar would love some. As long as he doesn't drink my share too." He teased.

Ivar sighed, "I like mead… Especially good mead. Not my fault."

"You are more than welcome to join us for the harvest festival." Adania smiled at them.

Once they were done with breakfast, she walked out of the longhouse with them and walked down toward the first place they needed to go.

The hunter's hall was their first stop. Adania listened to the hunters and had to choose between boar or bear for the feast.

"Bear will be difficult but we would get more meat from it. The boar is still dangerous but we could drop a couple of them in place of one bear." One of the hunters explained.

Adania thought for a moment, "What would you suggest?"

"Honestly that is up to you Jarlskona. We will do what you decide."

Adania thought for a moment, "drop the boars. I don't want any of you getting hurt or worse."

"It will be done."

She smiled and nodded to the man.

"Stop two?" She looked at Runa.

Jerrick and Ivar just watched in awe of the two at how quick things were getting dealt with.

"Stop two would be the brewery."

"Of course, it is." Adania snickered. "Alright let's go… Do we need to take a break for you?"

Runa shook her head, "I'm fine Adania."

"Alright… I don't want you pushing yourself either."

"I'm fine. I promise."

The four walked down the pathways toward the brewery. "Yrsa? You in?" Adania called once they walked into the building.

A small portly woman in red and blue stepped out from a doorway. "Jarlskona… I didn't expect you today."

"I apologize Yrsa… I wanted to make sure that everything was going well for the harvest festival and see if you needed anything."

She shook her head, "I don't need anything. The Wolf mead is sitting and I'm making a few other ones as well."

"Would it be possible to send our visitors home with a bottle or two each of the Wolf mead?"

Yrsa thought for a moment, "I believe I have a couple of bottles to spare for them."

Adania smiled, "Thank you, and please don't hesitate to come find me if you need anything."

"Thank you, Jarlskona. I will be sure to find you if I need anything." The woman left to go back to work on the mead.

Adania nodded and turned to the other three. "What?"

Jerrick shook his head, "Nothing, just how you handle people..."

Runa snickered, "And to think she doesn't like dealing with many people."

Ivar and Jerrick looked at Adania, "Really?" Ivar cocked his head to the side confused. "You're such a natural at it."

She shrugged, "Probably because I watched my father do it for so long."

Runa shook her head, "I doubt that one. I'm sure Odin gave you the insight to deal with people."

"Stop three?" Adania put her hands on her hips and looked at Runa.

Runa sighed, "We can go to the bakery or we can go to the weavers."

Adania thought for a moment, "the weavers probably... We need to make sure that we have all the fabric we're going to need or any trim and whatnot."

"Onward then." Runa walked with Adania down the pathways branching toward the weaver's hut.

"Astrid?" Adania called once they were close. Fabric hung on lines to dry in varying colors of red, orange, and yellow. Some trim hung on smaller lines, most likely they were freshly washed.

"Jarlskona? I didn't expect you today." Astrid spoke softly and came around from the back of the building wiping her hands. Her apron a mess of colors.

"You seem to be working hard."

"As always. I can't slack off it seems." She laughed some then.

Adania smiled, "I hope you're getting some sleep in between all the things you're doing."

"I am, and I have help this year with the fabric and the trim. Some of our newer clansmen have joined me in crafting and dying fabric. Having one of the males around is a huge help when it comes to getting the fabric out of the dyes considering how heavy some of that gets. Especially the canvas."

"Well, if you need any help. Please don't hesitate to come ask and I will come help if I can or I will find you someone who can."

"Thank you. Jarlskona." The blonde sighed. "I need to get back to it. These fabrics aren't going to make themselves."

"Thank you, Astrid. You're definitely a gift from Frigg."

"It's my pleasure." She smiled sweetly and headed back toward the back of the building.

"I think next would be Hrafn at the aviary."

Runa nodded. "You would be correct my dearest Jarlskona."

Adania sighed, "Runa, please don't start with me today, it is way too early to deal with your shenanigans."

Runa snickered, "I gotta give you shit somehow since I can't give it to you in a friendly fighting match."

Adania shrugged then and walked down the pathways toward the aviary.

"Hey! Hrafn? You here?" Adania called as she walked into the hut and looked around.

A tall man came into view from a doorway. "Jarlskona, it's nice to see you."

"Nice to see you, as always." She smiled at him. "Do you need anything since we're getting ready for the harvest festival?"

He shook his head as a raven landed on his shoulder. Petting the bird, he smiled at her. "I think I have everything taken care of here. If I need anything I will let you know."

Adania nodded and smiled again. "Such gorgeous creatures." she looked at him. "You take excellent care of them."

"I do try. And thank you for checking in on us."

"Of course." she nodded and with that, the four of them left.

Ivar and Jerrick still in tow. "Seriously, the way you deal with people is astounding." Ivar commented, "Jerrick doesn't even deal with people that well, and he's been at this for years."

Jerrick hit Ivar in the chest, "Rude ass."

"Are you boys ready for the next one or do I need to let you sort out this whole thing before we go anywhere else?" Adania teased and snickered.

"We're good," Jerrick spoke before Ivar could say anything.

"Good, then onward we go."

Adania grinned and started to walk further throughout Jokolvikra.

She stopped at the stables, the farms, the tanner's, the tattoo shop, the shipyard, trading post, fishing hut, blacksmith, and jewelry makers, before finally making it back to Randvi's hut and longhouse.

"That would be the sights and people of my home." Adania looked at the two males that accompanied her and Runa.

Runa was very much winded and sat down on a crate in front of the longhouse.

"I told you not to overdo it."

"I didn't think I was." Runa looked up at her friend.

"Just wait until you have a baby. I'm sure you will be the same way."

"I would need a man for that first."

Runa grinned, "I'm sure you could ask Ivar or Jerrick."

Adania scowled at Runa.

Jerrick and Ivar laughed then, "what would be the conditions on getting your hand anyway?"

Adania sighed and looked at Jerrick who had asked, "You would have to beat me in hand-to-hand combat... I want to make sure that you could protect me better than I protect myself."

Runa piped up then, "Originally you would have to fight me but since I have a baby growing," Runa shrugged, "I'm not eligible to fight you guys."

Jerrick looked at Adania, "No offense, but I have heard how Wolf clan fights, and I don't think I could handle you."

Adania and Runa laughed. "There are few who can handle Wolf clan women." Adania grinned at him.

Ivar shook his head, "I've seen how you fight and I don't think I could handle it either."

Runa looked at both of them, "I didn't know Serpent men were such babies." she teased.

Jerrick looked at Runa then, "Not babies as much as we know when we're outmatched."

Adania looked at the males, "We could always just have a friendly sparring match."

Jerrick and Ivar looked at each other and shrugged, "What do you think Jerrick?"

"We can give it a go."

Adania grinned mischievously, "Don't say I didn't warn you."

"I have a feeling that she's gonna kick our asses," Ivar smirked at Jerrick.

"That's alright... I haven't had my ass kicked in a really long time." Jerrick responded.

CHAPTER 7
CREATIVITY

"To create and try new things."

Adania stood overlooking the festival activities. Ivar and Jerrick had joined them a few days prior to the festival beginning to add a couple extra sets of hands in setting up.

"With everyone here and gathered around. We've had a bountiful harvest this year and we will be fed through the winter months. This festival is a thank you to the gods that have granted us such things. Make sure to thank Freyr and Sif with a horn of mead and an offering." Adania raised a horn and drank from it.

"Skal!" Everyone responded and drank from their own cups and horns.

There was archery, drinking contests, a couple of skalds were singing and telling stories, kid's activities, and shopping in the marketplace.

Adania made sure to walk around and see if anything was needed or if anyone needed help. She was told that she should be enjoying the festival and not to worry about anything.

Watching Ivar and Jerrick laughing and drinking made her giggle to herself. Runa was on a bench doing some embroidery and teaching some of the kids to do it as well.

Adania went to a large tree that lay in the middle of Jokolvikra.

"I hope you're taking care of yourself father." She whispered softly and a cool breeze blew her hair gently and she could have sworn she heard her father's voice saying to go have fun.

Smiling to herself she went back to the festival and decided she would try the archery targets and did fairly well. Though, naturally, one of the hunters won the archery competition.

She also involved herself in Runa's embroidery lessons and one of the drinking contests which she failed at both.

Laughing, she sat at a table talking to Jerrick and Ivar.

Runa walked over to her and put her hands on her hips. "Adania... You don't normally involve yourself in festivals. You normally sit there watching everyone else having fun. What took the stick out of your ass?"

Adania looked up at Runa, her face slightly flushed from drinking. "I figured why not? I wanted to try something new."

Runa looked at her skeptically. "Uh-huh... I don't believe that... Which deity told you to go have fun? Was it Loki? It was Loki, wasn't it?"

Adania shook her head slightly. "No. No Loki. I went to the big tree that we used to climb on as kids and thought I heard my father's voice so I decided to just let loose a little bit."

Runa looked at her Jarlskona and smiled, "I know you miss your father. I miss him and my own too, but if talking to him in Valhalla makes you feel better and he answers then I'm not going to judge. Though your old man is probably far more drunk than you are."

"I'm not drunk... I'm happily... fuzzy."

"Fuzzy?" Runa looked at her with an eyebrow raised.

Adania nodded. "Yea... Like a bear pelt."

Runa sighed and put her hand to her face. Looking at Jerrick, who was the most sober out of the three of them, she said, "Make sure gets to bed and doesn't stay up too late. Also, she's going to need some water too. No more mead for a while."

"Runa..." Adania whined. "But it's Wolf mead... And it's so good."

"You need water too, Adania. We don't need our Jarlskona puking up her insides in the morning... or even later this evening because she's been drinking too much."

"Okay... Fine. I'll drink water... Once I finish this cup." She giggled which made Ivar laugh.

Jerrick and Runa both sighed. "These two are going to need help, aren't they?" Runa asked looking up at Jerrick.

"Most likely." Jerrick sighed as he looked at Adania and Ivar.

"Adania normally doesn't drink enough to get this way... but she has been dealing with a lot."

Once Adania's cup was empty Runa grabbed some cold water and brought it to her.

Several hours later, the entire Wolf clan and all the guests they had were in the longhouse eating.

Adania was holding her head and trying not to groan at how loud everything was.

Runa handed her another cup of water.

"Ugh... Gods... I feel like my head is splitting apart."

Runa sighed, "That happens when you drink like you were."

"Don't ever let me do that again."

"Let this be a lesson you learn on your own... It was nice to see you participate in the festival though. I'm sure everyone else enjoyed having you around too. You're far more loved around here than you give yourself credit for."

"I pray that Eir makes this headache go away... Or Randvi gives me some kind of cure-all something or other..."

"Speaking of." Runa smirked.

Randvi was walking up with a small bowl. "I heard someone was drinking far more than she was used to."

"Please tell me that that will get rid of the pain in my head."

"It will... but it tastes pretty gross... and no I'm not telling you what's in it."

"Don't care... give." Adania sighed and took the bowl downing the remedy that was in it. Quickly grabbing the water, she chugged it. "Ugh... so gross."

"But give it a few minutes and it will help with the headache." Randvi stood there and looked at everyone having fun at the feast. "I will head back to my hut. I have a lot to do and a lot to get ready for... There are plenty more that are going to need that same remedy by the morning."

Adania sighed as she already was starting to feel slightly better. "Thank you, Randvi. I appreciate all that you do for us."

"You are welcome wolfling. I am happy to help. Any time that you need me I will be here."

Adania nodded and watched the woman leave. "There are times she scares me."

Runa laughed some then. "She's not so bad."

"Her always popping up randomly when she's needed... That's what scares me."

Runa shrugged. "She's always been like that... but she has a couple of apprentices now."

"Oh great... More that can somehow appear out of nowhere."

"Revna and Helga are learning from Randvi. They joined us from Serpent clan." Runa sat next to Adania.

"How is it that you know all of this?"

"Because I'm your hersir. It's my job to know things and take care of things behind the scenes for you. I try to make your job a little easier."

"You were truly sent by the gods." Adania smiled at Runa. "Is there anything I can do for you? You have done all of this for me and helped out on more than one occasion."

Runa shook her head, "As of right now. No. I'm perfectly fine... But I would like for you to help me take care of the baby once I have it... I think it's going to be a boy and if it is I was thinking about naming him Gunnar."

Adania smiled and nodded, "I think that's a wonderful idea."

Runa smiled and rubbed on her belly. She was finally starting to show that she was pregnant.

Adania hugged Runa. "If it's a girl?"

Runa shrugged, "I'm not sure honestly... Maybe Brenna or Torhild... I haven't thought about it."

Adania chuckled, "Well, we're going to try and keep you and the baby healthy."

Runa sighed, "If anything happens to me... Make sure you take care of the baby, okay?"

Adania shook her head, "You'll be fine Runa. Randvi and I will make sure of it."

Runa smiled and nodded, "I can see you aren't going to budge on this."

Adania shook her head, "Nope."

Runa sighed again, "Fine."

The festival was starting to settle down with families leaving and children falling asleep. All that remained were single adults and those that liked to drink.

Adania looked around and then hugged Runa, "I need to get to bed. I'm sure the festivities are going to go on well into the night and I don't want to deal with being exhausted tomorrow morning."

Runa nodded, "I'm going to be heading to bed myself. I hope we don't have too much of a mess to clean up tomorrow."

Adania grinned, "Well, for those that drink too much. I'll make sure to speak extra loud for them."

Runa laughed some, "There are times you are an ass."

Adania shrugged, "You wouldn't have me any other way."

Runa shook her head again, "You're right."

With that, the two headed back to their respective homes and went to bed.

The next morning, Adania awoke and left the longhouse. Stretching as she walked down the pathways toward the festival, she noticed some people still awake from the night before.

Shaking her head, she thought about how exhausted she would be if she did such things.

She met Runa by the large tree that was in the middle of Jokolvikra.

Small wooden plaques hung on ribbons with the names of those that had passed into the world of the dead.

"Let's go make sure that there hasn't been any fighting after we went to bed." Runa looked at Adania.

"There most likely was, but we weren't woken up so it shouldn't be too bad. I'm sure Ivar and Jerrick are around here somewhere."

Runa nodded, "looks like we have a couple of men to find." She grinned.

"No. No. No... I don't look at either of them like that."

"Jerrick or Ivar would make a good husband."

"I don't doubt it, but if they can't beat me in hand-to-hand combat then I don't want them."

Runa rolled her eyes, "Seriously Adania. You need to find a husband."

Adania shrugged, "The time will come when I get a husband, but now is not that time. I'm sure that Freyja will send me one when she decides that it's time..."

Runa went to say something and Adania went walking up to a table and slammed her hand on it. Ivar and Jerrick both jumped awake.

Ivar had been sleeping on the ground using a table-top one gallon mead barrel as a pillow and Jerrick fell asleep hunched over in the chair he had been sitting in.

Jerrick looked up at the woman squinting, "Jarlskona? It's morning already? I swear I just closed my eyes for a moment."

"You fell asleep after Runa and I went to bed. Which means you fell asleep late... Time to rise and shine and start the festivities again!" She yelled.

Jerrick and Ivar both held their heads in pain.

"Runa, can you go get Randvi... I'm sure she will need to bring that concoction of hers."

Runa nodded and went to walk away when she noticed Randvi walking toward the festival grounds with two other women, all of which holding a few of the one gallon barrels.

"Looks like she is already on it."

Adania looked up seeing the three, "Morning!" she yelled making the two males groan.

"You're doing this on purpose," Jerrick complained.

She gave a mock gasp, "Jerrick... I beg your pardon. I would *never*."

Jerrick got up from the chair and groaned as he stretched, "I hope she's bringing something for this headache."

Adania nodded, "That's what should be in the small barrels that they have. Though, I will warn you now. It's excruciatingly bitter and it tastes like absolute ass, but it works." She tapped his chest gently and went to Randvi to get a cup for Jerrick and Ivar.

"Try not to think about it and just drink it."

Jerrick drank it and let out a growl of disgust, "Ugh. Gods... What in Hel is that?"

"Wolf clan secret," Randvi smirked at him and then winked.

Adania gave a cup to Ivar who downed it and shook his head but didn't let out any kind of disgust as Jerrick had.

"Gross, but it is a medicine... At least I think it's medicine anyway... So being gross is to be expected."

Adania looked at them again. "Give that a few minutes to work and you should be feeling better in no time." she smiled and started to leave to go do activities she hadn't done yet.

She was enjoying herself and it would be a shame once all the guests left and they had to go back to normal life. She never really thought about how much fun she would have at a festival like she was.

Granted, she's had fun before at festivals when she and Runa were kids, but this was the most fun she could remember having.

It would be over in a few days and it made her sigh. The breeze went against her face. It was going to be a harsh winter. It was barely even harvest time and it was already quite cold.

She gave a silent prayer to Ullr to be forgiving this winter and then went back to the festival and its activities. Yule would be coming up in about three months.

There's another festival she would have to get ready for.

CHAPTER 8
PERSEVERANCE

"Giving up is not an option."

Adania stood in the rain. She had emptied her stomach a few times now. First her father, then Gunnar, and now Runa.

This year was deteriorating her mental fortitude in mass quantities. Between the raids and losing the last of the family she had left, she didn't know which was worse.

"Please welcome Runa into your halls Hel… She is a good woman and I think you will enjoy her company… Look after her for me." Adania wiped her face and sniffled slightly.

Sighing she went back into Randvi's hut after what felt like an eternity.

Randvi handed Adania a baby wrapped in a small blanket.

"Randvi… I can't… I'm unsteady and scared…"

"I know wolfling, and I will look after him for a while until you are ready… I know this is difficult for you. You lost three of your closest people in a year. The boy needs a name though. I will give him all the blessings of the gods I can to make sure he is healthy and strong. I will introduce him to the gods, as well as Gunnar and Runa, but he does need a name before I do such things."

Adania sighed and handed the baby back to Randvi, "Runa said if it was a boy, she would name him Gunnar after his father."

"Then I will present him to the gods and his parents as such." Randvi tapped Adania on the arm. "It will get better child. Odin has great things in store for you."

Adania shook her head, "I feel like I have angered the gods in some way and that they hate me."

Randvi sighed and looked at the young woman, "the gods don't hate you. These things happen. I know it is rough, but you will make it through and you will be a strong woman because of it... Again, myself, Revna, and Helga will look after him in the meantime." Randvi put the baby down in a crib on the floor within her hut before going back to Adania.

Adania looked at Randvi, "I need to go and clear my head. I'm dizzy and nauseous and my mind is a snowball running down the mountain."

Randvi nodded at her and hugged her, "I will be here. If you want to talk or vent or whatever you need."

Adania nodded, "Thank you Randvi."

"Anytime Adania."

The redhead smiled weakly and sighed before leaving the hut and going to the longhouse. She needed mead and a lot of it.

Several weeks had passed after Runa's passing and Adania seemed to just be going through the motions of her day-to-day activities.

She had been a mess and tried to do everything on her own without much help.

Adania sat up on a small hill that overlooked the village. Stones sat upon the dirt with names etched into the surface.

Ulf.
Audun.
Gunnar.
Runa.

Laying in the grass in a red apron dress and brown under-dress, she sighed and spoke to the stones softly. Closing her eyes and enjoying the feel of the breeze against her face, she almost fell asleep despite it being cold outside.

The first snow hadn't fallen yet but it was getting close.

The sound of the war horns startled her from her thoughts, "For the love of Thor…" She growled.

Sitting up, her eyes caught a glimpse of arrows flying over the village and longships off the shore with banners of red and black.

Looking up at the sky she cursed loudly to herself and called Loki many things, none of which were nice; let alone appropriate for a young lady to be saying.

Her mind now no longer on unconscious motions.

Adania was in her warrior mindset.

She had a village to protect.

Running into the village she passed one of the blacksmiths along the way and grabbed a sword and shield.

"Randvi, make sure everyone gets into the longhouse!" She yelled noticing the three seers as she came into the main thoroughfares.

"Yes, Jarlskona." Randvi nodded as Revna took Gunnar from the older woman.

"You're going to need help." Helga offered to Adania.

"I'll take all the help I can get." She smiled at the woman with whom she had been sparring with the last few weeks.

Adania began barking orders to the warriors she had. A few she sent to protect the longhouse and then the rest were with her.

Despite the calculated demeanor she presented, there was a silent rage deep within.

Just as the longships hit the docks, she and her warriors were already closing in.

A small group stayed around her.

Another volley of arrows shot from the longboats.

"Shields!" Adania yelled and all of them put their shields up over their heads to block the incoming arrows.

Warriors dressed in red and black stormed up the pathways and the clash began.

Now covered in blood and viscera she made her way to the one she assumed was the leader.

A man dressed in dragon scale tooled leather. Standing at six feet tall with long brown hair.

She knew she had seen this armor before.

'My dream...' Adania thought to herself as everything began to click into place. *'Freyja... You cheeky bitch...'* Panting from the fighting she had already been doing, she flung the shield at the man.

She gave a predatory growl at him.

"Awe, how cute. The little wolfling wants to play." He grinned at her as he smacked the shield from the air making it clatter to the cold, hardened dirt.

That voice, made her skin crawl but also gave a flutter deep in the pit of her stomach. He hadn't even yelled. He hadn't needed to.

He wasn't an imposing man like her father was.

Staring at the man in front of her covered in grime, blood, and sweat, his arms were not the thick corded tree trunks that many of the warriors sported, but instead was smaller, leaner, but his movements told her to not underestimate him.

He moved like a predator, a wolf. She was used to dealing with wolves and the way they moved but there was that aura he put off... Damn.

Definitely lived up to the dragon aspect in that regard.

"Are you making a challenge at me?" He seemed almost amused at the fact that she had thrown the shield at him.

"You can bet your sweet ass that's a challenge." She barked.

He chuckled, "Alright. What challenge might that be? Embroidery?"

The fighting around them had stopped and both clans stood watching the exchange.

Adania was fuming, "Just because I'm a woman doesn't mean I can't fight."

"I have heard the rumors of Wolf clan women. You'll stab a man as equally as you will sleep with one."

Okay, that remark was pretty true.

She certainly had no problem stabbing a man, especially with how pissed she was.

Adjusting her posture, she stood straight and crossed her arms over her chest.

"One-on-one, hand-to-hand combat, no weapons aside from fists and feet... best two of three."

"Think you can handle it, Wolf?"

She snorted, "You're about to get a lesson in how Wolf clan women are."

The male put his weapons in the dirt with his shield on top of them. "Alright, little wolf. Let's see how you can work me over." His voice was smooth and hypnotic as he let out another chuckle.

'Chastising bastard.' She thought to herself. Adania was not in the mood for dealing with this right now.

"But I will agree to hand-to-hand combat with you… If I win, I take what I want."

"*If* you win… If I win then you help rebuild and leave." Words just flowed out of her mouth without a second thought.

"I plan on rebuilding this place anyway." He gave her a cocky grin.

If she wasn't so angry, he would be attractive.

He was definitely a good-looking man.

Brown hair went down a little past his shoulders and was braided to keep it out of his face.

'I'm going to bury his face in the dirt…' she thought. "What are you looking at?" She barked at him.

"I'm looking at what I think is supposed to be a lady." He gave another smug grin.

Wait… She had heard that before. Where though?

'Ugh… Damn it all.' Her mind didn't want to cooperate with her, even in the slightest.

Rolling her eyes, she started to walk around him. He followed her movements with his own.

Neither of them wanted to make the first move.

Very quickly, Adania got bored and went after him. A punch to the face that he didn't block. That was going to bruise.

She was quite proud of herself. He definitely was going to feel it later.

"I was trying to be nice." His voice sent a shiver down her spine.

"Nice my ass." She spat.

He looked at her and then spit out some blood onto the ground, "I didn't quite expect you to hit me quite that hard."

She dodged out of the way from the punch he was throwing in her direction. Dropping to the ground she knocked his feet out from under him and pinned him to the ground. Struggling ensued and he managed to get her pinned.

One and one.

Moving under him she managed to take a fist and slam it into the side of his head making him recoil and groan. "Shit..." He growled and she threw him off of her.

Getting to their feet more punches were thrown and she got him on the ground where he quickly turned the pin on her.

Two and two.

Struggling to get out of his grip she growled and headbutted him as hard as she could.

In doing so, her own vision blurred.

'*Shit... not good.*' She thought to herself.

Trying to shake the darkness from taking her vision she managed to fight it. Though the minute she stood up, she crumpled to the dirt.

The man she had been fighting went over to her and caught her before she hurt herself.

"You definitely live up to the Wolf clan's fiery whirlwind of a temper." He said more to himself than to her.

He could feel the bruise on his cheek already starting, his head hurt, and he had a bloody lip to match the rest.

Picking her up, he sighed. "This village and clan are mine!" He yelled.

Dragon clan cheered.

All Wolf clan could do was just groan and sigh in unison.

"Someone take me to the longhouse so that we can deal with her."

With that, he was escorted to the longhouse by a few of the wolf clan members.

Randvi, Revna, and Helga went to her room and changed her out of her bloody clothes, and cleaned her face and hair with the male waiting outside the room until they were done.

"Try to wake her now and then to make sure she is alright," Randvi spoke to him once they had left the room. "She has been changed and cleaned up, do treat her with care." She scolded.

The male nodded, "of course."

Several hours passed before the fiery redhead awoke with a headache that made everything around her blur and made her want to puke. "Ugh... Gods... Why do I feel like I've been run over by a cart..." She said clutching her head and trying to steady herself as she stood.

Groaning she fell against a strong chest. Looking up at him, the fight started to replay itself in her mind.

"Why in Helheim are you in my room?"

"I was taking care of you after our fight. I must say... You have a punch that nearly knocked me on my ass."

She noticed she was in new clothes and was clean. A deep red blush covered her face. "You took care of me?! You saw me naked?! You changed my clothes?!" She pushed away from him only to have him steady her before she fell backward.

"No, your seers did all that. I waited in the hall and I took care of you after that."

She sighed as the dizziness began to slowly fade.

"Well... at least I have some dignity left."

He cocked an eyebrow at her.

"I lost a fight..."

"You put up a damn good one..." he said rubbing his cheek and jaw that was already bruising.

"I guess you're not used to effervescent women?"

"That's one word for it." He chuckled and it made her heart stop.

Pale sea kissed skin, a band of gold about his head and eyes as green as a gemstone. A strong but angular jaw set in a scowl in thought and the midnight of a beard covering his chin

'Is this what mother felt like with father?' She sighed as she thought about her parents, and the love they had for one another... or at least what she remembered of them.

His voice interrupted her thoughts, "I am Brynjolf by the way..."

"Adania... I guess I get to be the one to show you around Jokolvikra then... Since you won our fight." She sounded almost sad.

"I will take the village as mine yes... but I'm going to need a strong woman to fight beside me." He gave her a half-cocked smile.

"Is that your way of saying you want me as your wife?" Adania blinked a few times in disbelief.

Brynjolf looked at her and chuckled, "If that is something I can do. I haven't had anyone actually hold up against me before... You've been the first one not afraid to punch me. I'm used to women who are far more... Fairer? I guess is the word. Especially the higher-ranking families in my clan. Many of them just want to sit around and do embroidery or sewing... None want to spar with me or get dirty... Let alone spar with me while rolling around in the dirt." He chuckled.

"You have one fight with me and you want to marry me?" Adania still seemed confused. Green eyes met his own and she felt like he was peering into her very existence.

"You're strong. You pack one Hel of a punch. You were fighting on the front lines with your people. That says a lot about your character as a leader."

She shrugged then, "My people depend on me and it's my duty to protect them."

"Exactly, you don't run in terror the minute that you're invaded... You run towards it. You threw a shield at me and challenged me to a one-on-one for the sake of your people." He smiled. "And that's exactly what I want in a woman. Someone who is going to fight beside me and protect our people just as much as I will."

Blushing slightly, she smiled and nodded, "On one condition Brynjolf."

"Name it." He spoke without hesitation.

"You fix the mess you made of my village."

He snickered to himself and nodded, "It's going to be our village now."

"I still can't believe I lost to you though. It bothers me a bit... Tradition in my family is women who are beaten in hand-to-hand combat marry the one they lose to."

He cocked a brow at her, "Oh?"

"We're trained from the time we are old enough to hold a sword or ax... whatever our preferred weapon turns out to be... And if we're beaten that means that that man can protect us better than we can protect ourselves and strong enough to look after the family."

"Oh... That makes sense. It's different from the things most women are taught... At least from what I have seen anyway."

CHAPTER 9
Loyalty

"To trust and believe in and devote ourselves to others."

Adania spent the next couple of weeks getting to know Brynjolf better. He offered to sleep in her old room while she took the Jarl's room in the meantime, even though he had asked for her to marry him. She was surprised at how much his attitude had changed compared to the raid, but then again it could have just been a battle lust. That's what she blamed anyway.

He was always checking on her to make sure that she was still feeling alright after she smacked his head as hard as she did.

"Brynjolf… I'm fine. I promise. Gods, you dote on me anymore and I'm going to throw you into the water at the docks to straighten your head out." She teased.

He grinned at her, "not before you fall into the water with me."

Shaking her head, she pushed him away from her gently, "So either you can go around and see if anyone needs anything… Since you are going to be their new Jarl… *or* you can come with me and start planning a hand-fasting…"

He thought for a moment and kissed her forehead. "I will let you handle all the hand-fasting shit… It's more a day for you than it is for me anyway."

Adania shook her head, "I want you involved too... After all, I never even thought I would have a husband... I have no idea how to even *begin* planning this thing."

He put his hands on her cheeks and smiled at her, "I have all the faith in you, Elska."

"Alright. Fine... but you *will* be helping at some point. I'm not doing everything by myself."

He sighed with his hands on his hips as he stood looking down at the dirt before looking at her. "Fine. I will help on some things but whatever you want you can have."

"Bryn!" she hit his chest playfully causing him to rub his chest as if she had hurt him.

"My lady... You are so violent... My poor little body will bruise."

She rolled her eyes and looked at him, "Poor little body my ass."

He grinned and turned her around pushing her gently. "Go take care of what you need to. I'll meet you in the feast hall this evening."

"What colors do you want to wear?"

"Surprise me, Addy." He had taken to calling her such, which was odd for her but she was getting used to it. The only other person to call her 'Addy' regularly had been her father.

She groaned, "You are impossible..."

"The gods put me on this world *just* to irritate you." He leaned against her ear and kissed her temple.

The short, well-kept beard brushed against her skin making her rub her face, "alright fine."

"I'll see you later this evening." Brynjolf patted her on the small of her back as he turned to go elsewhere.

She sighed to herself and shook her head before walking toward the weaver's hut to look at fabric, trim, and anything else she might need.

Astrid was frantically running around when Adania walked in.

"Astrid... You are running around like a chicken with no head. Can I help at all?"

"Jarlskona... I hate to be a bother."

"It's not a bother at all. What troubles you?"

"I have fabric to make and trim to do and on top of that I have to get ready for your hand-fasting and make sure all of that is done and dealt with and I feel like I'm running behind on everything.

Adania chuckled and looked at the woman. "I'll help out however I can and we can chat on the details of the hand-fasting."

Astrid nodded. "Sounds good to me, Jarlskona."

Adania shook her head. "Please, just call me Adania."

Astrid cocked her head to the side confused.

The redhead looked at Astrid and sighed. "I've never been a fan of using titles when not doing my duties. I want everyone to think of me as an equal when I'm out and about with all of you."

Astrid nodded again. "I can understand that... I will do my best to remember."

Adania smiled. "That's all I can ask for... So, what can I do?"

Astrid grabbed an apron that was coated in a plethora of colors and handed it to Adania.

Adania took it and put it on. Luckily, she was in a blue under-dress and a black apron dress. In case she did get dye on her it most likely wouldn't show on her clothes.

"What colors were you thinking about for your hand-fasting anyway?"

Adania shrugged to herself. "Honestly... I haven't got a clue. Brynjolf said to surprise him... Which doesn't help me much. His clan colors are black and red... Ours are blue and gray... So, I thought about finding a way to combine the colors somehow."

Astrid looked at Adania as she went to a large barrel to pull out fabric from the dye. Adania went to the other side to help her.

"I don't know how you do this by yourself all year round." Adania groaned slightly trying to help move the wet linen.

"You get used to it after a while. I normally have people to help me but they all seem busy today."

"Too busy to help you work? That seems counterproductive." Adania followed Astrid to the drying racks where she hung the drying fabrics, yarns, and threads.

"I'm used to doing most of the work since my husband died. He normally would help me move the wet fabric or help me get it dyed or whatever else I needed to have done here in the shop."

Adania sighed putting her hands on her hips as she watched the woman adjust the fabric to dry properly and evenly.

"So… You said you wanted to find a way to combine the colors of the clans to make your hand-fasting."

Adania nodded. She would have to talk to Brynjolf about having people help Astrid more often.

"Let's head in and get some more fabric in the dyes and we can talk while working."

Adania nodded and smiled at her, "sounds good to me Astrid, and thank you for this."

"It's not a problem, Adania. After all, I did the fabrics and trim for your parent's hand-fasting and I did the same for when you were born. I think it's tradition, at this point." Astrid shared a laugh with Adania then.

"I guess you're right."

"I have been at this for years after all."

Adania went back inside the building with Astrid and helped with moving fabric to the dye as well as yarn and thread.

"Brynjolf's clan colors are red and black, yes?" Astrid asked as she stirred the dye before grabbing bundles of thread and yarn.

"Yes," Adania answered and watched Astrid work as she held a bundle of fabric.

"I think we can put you in a red dress and him in a gray tunic. We can also put you in gray trim and him in red or black trim to keep with the blending of the two clans."

Adania nodded. "Sounds like a plan to me, Astrid… I'm going to have so much embroidery to do on these too."

Astrid looked at Adania, "From what I remember, you're not the greatest when it comes to embroidery."

Adania shook her head, "No, that was always Runa's thing… I would rather have a sword in my hand than a needle."

Astrid nodded, "Well if you want help, I can show you. I've done a good bit of it. Or you can talk to Randvi. She does a lot of it too, though she won't like to admit that her work is as pretty as it is."

A few more weeks passed and Adania was busy working on the fore-cloth that would be hanging between her brooches over her apron dress.

Many times she stabbed herself in the finger and much cursing came out of her mouth each time she did so.

Her dress was going to be red. The trim that lined the top and bottom was a woven pattern of a dark gray and then a light gray. The fore-cloth was a light gray with a black dragon in the middle.

Brynjolf's tunic was a light gray with black trim. Blue wolves adorned the chest piece.

More cursing filled the longhouse as she worked on the embroidery. "Definitely giving my blood to the gods for this..." She sighed. Her fingers had been pricked several times in the last few hours.

Brynjolf was away from the longhouse at her request so she could work in peace without his asking what she was doing or working on.

Though his voice would probably have eased her frustration rather than the needle she currently hand in hand.

Giving a disgruntled sigh, she picked up the fabric and took it to her room to hide it away from Brynjolf's eyes.

Once satisfied that it was hidden well enough, she left the longhouse to go check in on Astrid and several others to see if they needed help.

She needed to be out away from the longhouse for a little while to take a break from the embroidery... Plus, her fingers needed the rest.

Adania asked if anyone needed help and she was told, more often than not, that she needed to relax and get ready for her hand-fasting instead of worrying about work.

'For the love of Thor. No one is letting me do anything.' She thought to herself and let out an elongated sigh. "Brynjolf gets to work and he's going to be my husband," Adania said aloud to herself as she walked throughout the village.

Jokolvikra was getting larger than she was used to, and houses were being built quickly as the clan expanded.

It was getting colder and the snow would be falling almost at any time. She hugged herself tightly, pulling the coat and fur up to try and cut the cold from hitting against her skin, as the wind whipped past her.

"Alright, alright... I'll go back inside and continue working on that damn embroidery." She spoke softly looking up at the massive tree that sat in the middle of the village.

"Elska, what are you doing out here? Don't you want to be curled up in the longhouse by the fire?"

Brynjolf's voice came from behind her making her turn to look at him.

"My hands were getting tired of working on part of my dress... I needed a break so I thought I would walk around and see if anyone needed help."

"Sweet Addy." He smiled and kissed her forehead. "Go back-"

She cut him off, "If you tell me to go back inside and relax because of the hand-fasting, I'm going to punch you. I have heard that so much today..."

He laughed some then, "Alright fine. I won't tell you to go back and relax. What are we going to have for dinner? Is that better?"

The man standing to Brynjolf's right and slightly behind him was Ulfric. A blonde-haired, blue-eyed, barrel-chested male. He was always around Brynjolf much like Runa had been for her. His second in command.

"Ulfric and I just finished making the rounds with everyone. I'm wanting you to focus on the hand-fasting. Let me worry about the work that needs to be done and take some of that stress off of you."

Ulfric snickered, "You two aren't even married yet and she already has you wrapped around her finger."

"A finger I will gladly stay wrapped around." Brynjolf looked at the blond.

Adania blushed and punched both of them in the shoulder and went back toward the longhouse.

Brynjolf and Ulfric both rubbed their shoulders, "You just pissed off my bride-to-be."

Ulfric just shrugged, "Not my fault."

Brynjolf just shook his head, "There are times you are such an ass."

"I kind of have to be, especially when you're busy with your lady. Someone has to handle your clan when you can't."

Adania went back into the longhouse and began to work on dinner.

"Chicken? Beef? Pork? Lamb? Fish..." She sighed and thought momentarily about it.

Deciding on a leg of lamb with garlic butter and honey-glazed carrots she began to grab what she needed and began to cook.

Having some extra time on her hands, she made a simple bread while the lamb cooked.

Brynjolf walked in and was met with the smells of herbs and food. "That smells intoxicating, Addy. Those that feast in Valhalla should be jealous of your cooking and that they don't get to eat such good food."

She looked up at him then, "you sir, are a suck-up."

He grinned, "you're not mad at Ulfric?"

"No, I wouldn't say mad exactly. Embarrassed more like, I guess." She shrugged and continued to knead the dough before cutting it into smaller pieces to make small loaves for the both of them.

Brynjolf walked over to her and kissed her cheek, "can I help at all?"

"I think I got dinner covered. Though you could wash up dishes afterward... and wash yourself up now so that you're not tainting your mouth with dirt and grime alongside my cooking."

He chuckled to himself, "Of course, Addy." Going to a bucket filled with water and soap, he washed up his hands and face. Taking the bucket outside he went to go refill it with a small stream behind the longhouse toward the base of the mountain.

He came back several minutes later with fresh water and the soap in the bucket.

"Fresh water, like you asked." He walked up behind her and hugged her kissing against her ear and neck.

"Bryn!" she snickered, "I'm trying to cook dinner."

"Can I have you for dinner?"

She rolled her eyes and turned to look at him, "You are going to have to wait to have me."

He put his forehead against hers. "Fine, but you're not running away from me once we're married."

"I don't doubt it." She teased. "But dinner is almost done..."

The half-cocked smile that graced his face made her heart flutter.

He definitely had a way about him. The way he carried himself and the way he dealt with people all day. She would have to ask him how he came to be so good at it.

He always made it seem so effortless and she loved that about him.

CHAPTER 10
Simplicity

"To be natural and traditional, to be humble."

The day of the hand-fasting came faster than Adania had anticipated. She was excited, nervous, flighty, and even panicky.

Things hadn't even really started and she was already stressed.

Brynjolf and Adania decided to stick to tradition on *almost* everything.

It was going to be held on Freyja's Day.

Everything started the morning before the hand-fasting. Adania hadn't paid much attention to the overwhelming advice the other women were giving her on how to be a wife, a lover, or a mother. She was already nervous and overwhelmed with the planning, she felt like she was drowning.

Brynjolf would be off supposedly grave robbing an ancestor's grave or tomb.

Adania didn't know much about the male side of things and what was going to be happening with him.

She was dragged out of bed by her married female friends and was rushed around to get dressed, her hair done, and everything else that needed to be done.

Adania would have given Brynjolf her father's sword as a symbol of him being the protector rather than her father, but that had been put on the boat with him that she shot the flaming arrow on. She would have to find something else, and she knew exactly what to pick; a shield that her mother gave to her father hung in the longhouse above the fireplace in the Jarl's bedroom.

After the ceremony would be the feast.

The morning of the hand-fasting, Astrid helped Adania into her dress. She was stunned at how beautiful it had turned out and hugged Astrid tightly.

Yrsa put a bridal crown on Adania's head made of silver and gems from the mountain.

White wolf fur adorned her shoulders and clipped to her brooches where her treasure necklaces hung.

Adania really hoped that the celebration didn't last a week like some of the hand-fastings she had heard about.

They would be having boar for the feast, an animal sacrificed to Freyr and Freyja. The god of virility and prosperity and his sister, the goddess of love, sex, and fertility.

This was something that she hadn't thought about until now. '*I chose the animal without even really thinking about it when the hunters had asked about it…*' She thought silently to herself.

Already she was exhausted, she had stayed up late the night before to try and finish the embroidery on the cloth that hung on the outside of her dress. The tips of her fingers hurt just even thinking about it. It wasn't perfect by any means but she did it and she liked how it had turned out.

Trying to calm her nerves was hard. She would be married in a matter of hours and then be expected to be a wife, a leader, and a lover. Where would she find the time?

'*I'll just figure it out on my own I guess…*' she sighed and looked at the women around her.

"I'm happy that I get to share this day with my clansmen. You all have been Odin sent. I appreciate every single one of you and everything that you have done for me."

All the women hugged her. They walked her out of the room and to the front of the longhouse toward the large tree where Brynjolf, the gothi, and everyone else were waiting.

Brynjolf saw her and his mouth about dropped to the dirt.

It was cold and she was now rethinking about having the ceremony outside. Maybe they should have done this inside the longhouse.

'Too late to change it now.' She thought.

"May Odin give them knowledge and wisdom on the way to come. May Thor bless this union with strength and courage. And may Loki never deny them laughter... Bring forth your gifts to one another."

Brynjolf presented a sword to her. "This sword was my father's. I want to entrust it to you to give to our son."

She took it happily and gave it to one of her handmaids for the time being.

Taking the shield and presenting it to him, she smiled up at him. "I don't have my ancestral sword to give you as you have given me. However, I have my father's shield which I will entrust to you in order to protect our family and yourself."

He gave a half-cocked, charming smile and looked at her. Handing the shield to one of his attendants, he looked back at her with a wink.

Then, the gothi had Adania and Brynjolf take each other's wrists. He began wrapping braided ribbons of red and gray around their wrists and forearms as he spoke again. "As I wrap these ribbons, it spiritually ties you to one another. Will you share in each other's pain, joy, and dreams? Will you honor, respect, and protect one another?"

"We shall." Adania and Brynjolf looked at each other as the gothi spoke. She was no longer nervous, and there was a calm she now had that she hadn't had before.

"Brynjolf of Dragon clan. Do you swear before the gods on this day that you want to take this woman as your wife?"

"I swear." His voice was smooth like always.

"Adania of Wolf clan. Do you swear before the gods on this day that you want to take this man as your husband?"

"I swear."

Adania and Brynjolf turned to face the gothi as he used some of the boar blood to put runes on both of their foreheads.

"By the power of the nine realms and the acknowledgment of our mighty All Father. I pronounce you Viking and Valkyrie."

There were some chuckles among the people there, including Brynjolf and Adania.

"Kiss her already, you oaf."

Brynjolf leaned his forehead against hers and put his hand against her cheek, his thumb grazing over her cheekbone.

Snow began to fall with a bitter wind blowing through the village.

She leaned up the rest of the way and kissed him wrapping her arms around him.

"Skal!" Everyone cheered.

Adania pulled away blushing a soft pink. "Race you to the longhouse."

"We're not that far from the longhouse. Can't we-"

Adania didn't even let him finish before she took off running, laughing the entire time.

Brynjolf sighed tipping his head back with his hands on his hips, *"And* she's gone…" He said to himself and then started running up behind her.

Catching up to her he picked her up, turned her around, and tossed her over his shoulder.

"Brynjolf! Put me down!" She laughed and hit him against his back.

"Not a chance in Helheim." He grinned and slapped her on the backside.

"Brynjolf!" Adania squeaked.

He chuckled to himself and put her down just inside the longhouse on the wooden floor.

"Let's get the feast started and then tonight, you're mine." He whispered in her ear letting out a soft growl.

She blushed a deep scarlet and released a breath she hadn't realized she had been holding.

Everyone started to come into the longhouse not long after.

Adania and Brynjolf stood by the doorway receiving gifts.

One of Brynjolf's clansmen, Hillevi, kept giving Adania a look of seething fury.

Adania decided she would take care of that later. She wasn't going to let this take away from her and Brynjolf.

Once they had gotten everyone inside and everyone seated, Brynjolf stood holding a large cup of mead. "I am not one for speeches, as I prefer shoving food in my mouth, but I will say this. Yesterday, we were two clans. Today, we are one. We will forge new traditions and new generations."

With that, he drank from the cup as everyone cheered and yelled.

Adania smiled up at him, watching him in awe.

Brynjolf sat down and took her hand as servants brought out their feast that Adania had tried to help with earlier but had gotten shooed out of the kitchen.

Unlike most clans who had thralls, Adania's had actual servants. Paying them in fabric, gems, silver, amber, etcetera.

The party went on for several hours. Eating, drinking, dancing, and games went well into the night.

Families went home once the children started to fall asleep, others stayed in the longhouse drinking, and once everything settled down Adania and Brynjolf went up to what was now *their* room.

Adania was yawning as they walked up to the bedroom.

Upon reaching the door, she sighed and walked in, throwing herself on the bed with a soft coo.

Brynjolf bit his lip as he watched her move. "Addy… you have no idea how beautiful you truly are." He let out a soft purr-like noise. "We need to get you undressed if you intend to sleep on this bed. I don't think you want your brooches poking you all night."

Adania sat up and sighed. "You're right." Getting up she walked over to where she hung up her clothes, she unhooked her brooches from everything and set them down on a nightstand with the treasure necklaces with them.

The white wolf pelt shawl was tossed to the floor along with her apron dress as she stepped out of her shoes.

Brynjolf chuckled to himself. "Not quite what I meant but that works." Sitting on the bed, he stripped off his shoes and then his tunic tossing it to a chair nearby.

Adania admired the way his muscles moved in the candlelight. A few scars covered his torso, some very apparent they were from weapons, while others seemed to be from animals or other tools.

Crawling back onto the bed she traced a scar along his back. "How did you get this one?"

"Our first night together as an official couple and you want to know stories of my scars…" He teased and looked at her from over his shoulder.

"Sorry, I'm nervous… If I'm being honest…" She blushed a deep red and looked at him.

Smiling up at her, he sighed. "I was in a raid… I don't even remember what clan it was, and a man with an ax came up behind me and hit me with it. If it wasn't for Ulfric and my armor I wouldn't be here…"

Adania smiled and kissed his shoulder. "Then I need to thank Ulfric for keeping you alive this long." she teased.

He looked at her with a smile before tackling her to the bed making her laugh.

Biting her lip, she looked up at him. Her hair splayed out beneath her.

Wrapping her arms around his neck she pulled him down to her, kissing him deeply.

Brynjolf growled low in his throat sliding an arm around her.

Pulling away from her mouth he kissed against the hollow below her ear. His voice soft, "You tempt me, dearest." His hips easily fitting against hers and tortuously slow, he kissed along her skin. His teeth grazed her flesh every so often. He reached up and plucked at her nipples through her under-dress.

He needed to mark her, take her, and make her his own. He growled against her lip and bit playfully at the curve, "I want to devour you, but I would like to take my time…"

Moaning softly, she closed her eyes and enjoyed his touch. Her body arched into his hand wanting more. Her hand went to the back of his neck and gripped in his hair. "Bryn… Don't tease." Her hips rolled upward against his.

His mouth watered at the idea that this woman was his.

All.

His.

Smiling to himself, he pulled away from her again and gave a throaty laugh at her groan of protest.

Moving toward her feet and grabbing the bottom of her under-dress, he pushed it up slowly as he kissed up her leg to her thigh, giving soft bites occasionally against the exposed skin.

He growled low and nuzzled into the juncture of her thighs. His breath was hot over her core. He paused and stared up her body as she squirmed and whimpered. He waited until her eyes locked on his before slowly licking up her core to her clit.

He gripped her hips and held her right where he wanted her.

Adania's breath hitched. "Bryn..." her body shuddered. Her walls tightened as she squirmed under him. Groaning she rolled her hips against his mouth. "Brynjolf..." she groaned again and gripped in his hair tightly.

Wrapping her legs around his shoulders, she shuddered more. Her head turned to the side as she closed her eyes enjoying the feel of his mouth. "Don't stop..." she whispered.

Brynjolf smirked at the breathless moans coming from his shield maiden.

He licked up to her core one last time before creating a suction over her clit, the tip of his tongue flicking up and down against the sensitive nub as he did so. He loosened the grip of his right hand and teased the opening of her core with his finger.

He growled against her clit and slipped two fingers into her body, fingers curling in a come-hither motion.

Panting heavily, she rolled her hips in time with his fingers. "Brynjolf... fuck..." she groaned. Her walls tightened around his fingers and her nails scraped against his scalp as she gripped tightly into his hair. Shifting, she took her legs from around his shoulders and made more room for him between her thighs.

He bit down on her thigh before leaving a deep purple bruise as his fingers quickened their pace.

"Come for me... Don't worry, it'll be the first of many this evening." He went back to suckling her clit as he pushed her closer to the edge.

Throwing her head back, she arched against him.

Moaning loudly, she bit her lip and rolled her hips against his hand and mouth. Her breasts rose and fell in short bursts as she panted. "Fuck..." she groaned.

Her heart raced and her body felt heavy.

Tightening against his fingers again she whimpered. "Brynjolf..." she moaned. Her eyes went glassy and her body tensed. "There... Don't stop..." she moaned louder gripping into her own thigh and his hair again.

Rolling her hips more against his mouth and hands, she felt her body tighten and her walls clench tightly against his fingers.

Moments later, Adania felt her release. "Fuck... Bryn..." moaning loudly, her hips rode out her orgasm as she panted. "Shit..."

Brynjolf groaned as her body finally let go and tumbled off the edge. He didn't pull back until she was spent, body relaxing in the bed. He smirked and softly kissed the mark on her inner thigh.

He slowly kissed up her body as he slid off his pants, his arousal brushing along her wet core as he fused his lips with hers.

Kissing him in return, she wrapped her arms around his neck again.

Biting her lip, she felt his cock against her skin causing her breath to hitch. "You may not fit Bryn…" she whispered softly. "But you have gotten to taste me… maybe I should do the same for you." She winked. "Unless you just want to take me completely already." She grinned.

Squirming under him she pulled the under-dress off the rest of the way and threw it haphazardly to the floor.

He leaned down and captured a nipple in his lips, sucking on the peak, and pulling back with a soft pop, "oh if you wish to taste me, then, by all means, take control…"

Brynjolf laughed as she rolled him onto his back and began kissing down his torso, "And to think… You thought me a scoundrel a few weeks back…" he hissed as she bit down and laughed against the pain. "Okay… Okay point taken, I'll shut it."

His hand tangled in her hair softly, nails gently scraping her scalp. He had to gain control or she was going to get face fucked. He ground his teeth as she kissed closer and closer to his cock. "Easy Addy… I'm already strung tight."

She smirked and pushed him down to the bed as he leaned up on his elbows. Her nails raked across his stomach. "You're about to be worse." She smirked.

Before he could say anything, she captured his tip in her mouth.

Her tongue swirled against his skin. Her mouth stayed against his tip, teasing, as her hand went and began to stroke him.

After a few moments, she slid further down his cock with her mouth.

Her hand still stroking where her mouth wasn't. She pulled back slightly and let his tip pop out of her mouth.

She rolled her tongue against his tip before going to the base and licking from base to tip on the underside of his shaft. Capturing his tip again she slid as far as her small mouth would allow.

Grinning to herself, she started to slide up and down with her mouth slowly to tease before going faster and then slower again.

Brynjolf craned his neck as his head tilted backward. His mouth opened to let a deep groan slip from his throat. His right hand buried deeper into her locks of red as she tortured him so sweetly.

He winced as his hips bucked upward slightly as she began to move her mouth up and down the length of his shaft, "fuck Addy… S-Sorry…"

He growled low and sat up slowly to watch her work on his shaft, his pupils dilating at the sight. *'Oh, this woman is far too good for me…'* He thought to himself.

He panted hard as she got him just to the edge and then backed off.

Barking out a soft laugh, he hissed, "you dirty little wolf…"

Kissing him she started stroking him again before shifting and using her mouth again. Taking the entirety that she was able to with one stroke of her mouth, she started sliding up and down his cock faster than she had the first time as she stroked him more.

He was growling and grinding his teeth as she worked him into a mess.

Scraping her teeth ever so slightly just to send chills down his spine. Her hand went to his base as she let her mouth work. Going to the tip again, she worked her tongue against him feeling him twitch.

Preparing herself to swallow, she relaxed the muscles in her throat. Once his release hit her mouth, she swallowed what she could and pulled back from him licking her lips and smiling. "That was sweeter than I was expecting…" she grinned and sat up wiping her mouth.

She moved and positioned herself on his lap before starting to grind against him without him inside her yet.

He sat up on his elbows and watched her. His hands greedily wrapped around her hips as she ground her wetness against him. He smirked as she growled in his ear, "For the love of Thor, I would give you the moon if you let me, my love."

Brynjolf reached between them and angled the tip of his arousal against her core so when she rolled her hips forward, she took him in about half an inch. He growled low in his throat and bit her neck softly below her ear, "Do you wish to be in control this time?… If I am given the reigns, you will be fucked… Hard… and you will be sore tomorrow."

She bit her lip and thought for a moment. "This is going to be painful either way we go… but…" Leaning in she kissed him deeply and took his entire cock in one stroke.

Brynjolf groaned along with her as she took him in her core quick and swift.

Groaning loudly against his mouth she felt her walls tighten instantly against him. Pain roared through her body. "Fuck!" She growled against his mouth.

Panting loudly, she looked at him.

After several moments passed, she started rolling her hips against his now that her walls had relaxed.

His eyes rolled back as she began to move her body against him."I want you to take over." She groaned softly and kissed him again. "And if I end up sore tomorrow then you better make sure I can't leave the longhouse." She smirked. Leaning over she started nibbling gently on his neck to tease and started leaving hickeys against his skin.

His mouth melted with hers as she asked him to take over.

He braced her against him and quickly flipped them so she was on her back as his hips drove into hers. He growled and began at a quick and deep pace.

"Brynjolf…" she moaned softly. "Fuck…" Her hips instinctively rolled up against his trying to match his pace. Her walls tightened against his shaft making a loud moan escape her mouth again. Closing her eyes, she tipped her head back enjoying the feel of him.

She bit her lip, raking her nails down his back and arm making him bleed. She tried not to release yet but it was getting harder to do so.

His hands.

His teeth.

His cock.

Adania's brain and body were quickly becoming putty.

Groaning, she arched up against him pushing her breasts against his chest.

Brynjolf growled next to her ear. His right arm was above her head gripping the headboard as he drove his cock deep into her core. His left hand reached between their bodies and found the small nub between her legs, stroking it slowly and teasing at first. His hips grinding harshly into hers.

His own eyes rolled back at the feel of her body gripping his cock.

He let her ride that first wave to almost the point of coming.

He panted and nipped her ear as he fought his body for control, "I'm close my wolf."

"Bryn... Bryn..." She tapped his chest slightly. "I need a moment. Gods... I'm sorry."

He stopped and sat back on the bed. "Elska, are you in pain? Do you need water? Was I too rough?" His piercing green eyes showed concern.

Trying to catch her breath she sat up. "Brynjolf... I'm fine." she smiled and put her forehead against his. "I just needed a moment to catch my breath." She put a hand against his cheek.

Panting slightly, she waited for their bodies to cool but only slightly.

Looking at him in the moonlight; sweat covered, his cock coated in her fluids and blood.

Grinning, she pounced on him and took his cock again in one thrust, riding him hard this time.

Riding him hard until they both released.

Collapsing against him she panted heavily. Sweat covered her as she looked at him with a smile on her face. "How do you feel?" She teased as she nuzzled against his throat.

He chuckled as she collapsed into him and teased as she was born to do, "I feel good, are you able to walk still or shall I continue?"

She smiled and kissed him softly. "Give me a bit. I'm not done with you." She snickered and winked at him. Smiling she put her forehead against his again. "If I have my way, I'd take you all night if I am able... You may have created a monster." She snickered. "I love you, Brynjolf." She whispered softly and gave a sigh of contentment.

"I love you too, Addy..." His hands stroked her thighs slowly and his teeth grazed her shoulder softly, "but I am far from done with you myself."

CHAPTER 11
Discipline

"To stay true to the goals we have set as well as to our brothers and sisters while still remaining flexible."

Sunlight hit Brynjolf's face the next morning making him growl and roll over, his arms wrapping tightly around his woman.

Secure.

Safe.

He was sore in all the right places, his body covered in love bites and scratch marks… and he wouldn't have it any other way. He nuzzled her neck slowly and whispered, "Can you walk or must I break this bed to satisfy you?"

She giggled and rolled over to wrap her arms around his neck. "Morning." She smiled and kissed him softly. "I think I can walk… at least for now." She grinned. Shifting to get on top of him and straddle him, she looked down at him as her hair fell away from her face and down her back. "What's on your schedule for today? Anything important? Anything I can seduce you away from?" She teased.

Grinding against him slightly, she smirked before getting up. Her legs were slightly wobbly but soon she was able to adjust to walking again.

Brynjolf growled low at the playful teasing, the tempting, the tingle of anticipation was enough to draw a soft whimper from his lips, and then she got up and started dressing, "oh you sneaky little wolf."

He hopped out of bed and spun her around to kiss her deeply. "You'll be paying for getting me excited… but later."

She grinned at him and kissed him softly. "Let's go have breakfast and then I can work on training some of our people."

"Gods… Breakfast sounds so good right now." Holding his hand, she walked with him to the main part of the longhouse.

People were still there from the night before.

Upon walking into the feast hall many looked up and cheered at the couple.

This caused Adania to blush several shades of red as she gripped his hand tightly.

Brynjolf chuckled and kissed the side of her head.

She didn't expect this many people to still be here and she hadn't even braided her hair yet, let alone brushed it. She felt like she was a mess.

Brynjolf looked at everyone and shook his head. "Everyone out. I would like to have breakfast with my wife this morning with no one else to interrupt… So, go back home and eat. Quit drinking all our mead." He laughed some then and started to shoo everyone out as she stood back by the door they had entered from.

Once everyone was gone, he walked back over to her and kissed her softly. "There… Finally, some peace and quiet." He sighed.

She smiled up at him. "You are a Jarl and I am your Jarlskona… We don't get peace and quiet. Our clan is very much like our children. Always needing something." She grinned.

"You're not wrong, but I am sure that you are exhausted and in need of food and drink."

"No mead for me… Also, you will have to meet my child later."

He was taking a drink from a cup and almost spit the liquid in his mouth all over the floor. "You have a child? Why didn't that come up before?"

The panicked look on his face made her laugh. "I did not birth him, of course. His father died in a raid and his mother died giving birth to him. Randvi has been taking care of him until I felt ready to. Runa wanted to make sure he was taken care of." She sighed thinking about Runa and Gunnar. "They were the only ones I called my friends."

Brynjolf listened and hugged her tightly, "I'm sorry, Elska… I can't wait to meet him."

She smiled up at him. "He's only a couple of months old. Randvi has him and feeds him since she knows how to take care of babies better than I do... How about I take you to see him this afternoon after I train some of the young ones while you take care of all the duties that I hate doing?" She looked up at him innocently.

He groaned and sighed. "Alright, fine. I'll meet you at the training grounds this afternoon... The things I do for you." Brynjolf teased and sat down with her to eat breakfast.

After finishing breakfast and going back into the bedroom to do her hair, she came back opening the door to the longhouse to head to the training grounds, and noticed a thin layer of snow on the ground. The air swooped through the door making her suck in her breath.

It was frigid.

"I guess Ullr approves of our union... Or its my father looking down from Valhalla and he's upset." she chuckled and leaned up to kiss Brynjolf on the cheek.

Grabbing her coat made of wool, she put it on and headed out toward the training grounds.

Entering the training grounds, she sighed. Everyone was standing around talking and doing nothing.

"Hey! Quit messing around. We got a lot of work to do." Her voice was authoritative as she held a staff behind her head, her wrists hanging over the wood as she stood.

One of the dragon clan boys, who looked about seventeen, looked up at her. "What's it to you?" He mouthed off.

Adania sighed. "What's your name?"

He raised an eyebrow as he looked at her. "Tarben... Why?"

"You think you're hot shit? Prove it. Fight me... I'll even limit myself to this staff. You can pick up any of the weapons we have."

He went over to look at the arsenal of weapons that some of them had dragged out earlier. "If you think you can beat me. You lost to Brynjolf."

"Are you saying that you are better than your Jarl when it comes to battle? Because I highly doubt that one... He's also one of two that have beaten me. Let's see how well you do, Tarben."

He picked up an ax and a shield.

"Nice. Those are solid choices."

"These are all I fight with." His voice was cocky. "I'm the best of my age."

Adania chuckled. "Well, looks like I need to knock some sense into you then and have you learn something." She sighed and pretended to stretch.

This made him angry, "Take this seriously."

"I am. Come on then."

He lunged at her with the ax up above his head yelling the whole way.

She sighed and moved the staff to hook under the ax head; flinging the ax from his grip.

In one solid motion, she moved to trip him. The staff was against his chest as she pinned him to the ground. "Predictable…" Getting up, she helped him up from the snow.

Looking at the varying ages she would be helping train, she put the staff back on her shoulders behind her head.

"Wolf clan would learn to fight with all kinds of weapons, not just what we were good at. When you are on the field; you need to know how to use every weapon at any given point. Should you be disarmed like Tarben and you only know how to use a sword, or an ax, or whatever your favored weapon is. You cannot use the others effectively. So, starting today, you will learn how to use everything, starting with your worst one. A weapon is only as deadly as the one holding it. Even a shield can be a weapon if used as such. It is not used just to defend."

Tarben went over to the simple blacksmith tools on a bench and sulked that he had been so easily beaten.

Adania just continued her lessons.

Several hours went by when Brynjolf came up to the training grounds. She was sparring with some of the fighters all at once.

Brynjolf just watched her as she fought with a sword and shield. He was awestruck at the way she moved. Leaning against the fence, he smiled.

"Last night was your first time with a man… and you're still fighting like you're not in pain." He spoke once the sparring was over, as he didn't want to distract her.

"Oh no… I'm in pain. I just try not to let it bother me." She went over to him and kissed him softly. "Young Tarben learned a lesson earlier today. He's been sulking ever since."

"He'll get over it. He's not used to learning lessons the hard way… I assume you taught them all some valuable battlefield lessons?"

"To the best of my ability." She smiled at him then.

He motioned for Ulfric to continue the training, which the man did without complaint.

As the blond male passed the couple, he grinned, "He's always smiling when he watches you work or when you talk about something you love. It's good to see him smiling. He hasn't done so in a long time. Thanks for that Jarlskona."

Brynjolf scowled at Ulfric, "Shut your mouth. Ass."

She had noticed he did get touchy about some things; particularly if it involved his past.

Adania only shook her head at the two. It reminded her of how she and Runa had been less than a year ago, which brought her thoughts back to Randvi and the baby. "Can I take you to go to Randvi's hut? I'm hoping that Gunnar is awake this time. He's almost always sleeping when I go see him. I guess my free time always seems to coincide with his sleep."

Brynjolf looked at her. "Come on. Let's go see him, and you can tell me about him."

Adania held his hand as they walked over to Randvi's hut, "He looks more like his mother with his father's eyes. I named him Gunnar as per Runa's request before she passed…"

Entering into the hut, she looked around. "Randvi? I brought Brynjolf to see Gunnar."

Randvi came out from her back room. "I know dear child." She snickered and handed Adania the baby wrapped in a pelt to keep him warm.

"He's so small." Brynjolf looked at Gunnar and smiled.

"All babies are small, my dearest dragon." Adania teased and handed the baby to him to hold.

"I don't want to drop him."

"I normally sit with him and rock him or I sing to him. He seems to enjoy both at least."

Gunnar looked up at Brynjolf, cooed softly, and then yawned.

Randvi smiled. "Babies and infants spend most of their time still on the side of the ancestors, that's why they sleep so much."

Adania looked at her and nodded. "I wonder if he spends time with Runa or Gunnar."

Randvi smiled. "They are both most likely with Freyja in Folkvangr in the halls of Sessrumnir. I'm sure the Norn told Freyja what would happen with the two of them and Freyja hand picked Gunnar herself to protect her halls…" Randvi smiled as she looked at the couple. "Once we reach late childhood or early adulthood, most of us forget the lessons we learn from our predecessors in those infant times of sleep, though some of us end up taking those lessons without even realizing that that is what we are doing… But Gunnar will be a great help when you both have children. He will be closer to the second one that you will have."

Adania sighed and looked at the raven-haired woman. "I know your job is to be cryptic and mysterious but it gets tiring sometimes." She smiled at her.

Randvi shrugged. "Not my fault, young wolfling. I only give what the gods tell me too."

"I know."

Brynjolf handed the baby back to Randvi.

"Once everything has settled down around here, I will take him and take care of him like Runa had asked me to do. I feel like I can finally do so."

Randvi smiled. "If that is what you wish to do Jarlskona. Though, I would like to look after him until he hits one year. I have a feeling he will have a few health problems this winter and if he is here then the girls and I will be able to take care of it easier."

The winter months came and went fairly quickly considering how harsh it had been.

Almost every day Brynjolf and Adania would go their separate ways in the morning, he to carry out the duties of a Jarl and she would go train those that needed or wanted weapon training.

Winter was the easiest time to train since raids were almost nonexistent due to the conditions and it made travel difficult.

On top of training, Yule festival had everyone having fun and celebrating with twelve days of all kinds of activities. Songs, feasts, games, and drinking.

There was a tradition in Wolf clan that the Jarl go with the hunters to find an animal for the dinner feasts.

Brynjolf wanted to keep the tradition. Adania took him out with the hunters to teach him how to track and hunt the way they were taught to do so.

Finding a stag along the way, the group surrounded it and quickly took it down as silently as they could.

Brynjolf looked at them in amazement.

The group took the stag back to the village, finding another as they made the trek back.

Adania was given a bow by one of the hunters carrying the stag.

Silently, she stalked the doe. Once the opportunity rose, she pulled the bowstring back and let the arrow loose, dropping the doe.

Agnarr, one of the younger hunters went to go field dress the animal.

"Way to go, Addy." Brynjolf looked at her as she helped Agnarr with the field dressing.

She shrugged. "If I hadn't been born a Jarl's daughter I would have most likely joined with the hunters or the seers. I enjoy hunting a lot, don't get me wrong but I think I prefer to be on the battlefield."

Brynjolf chuckled slightly. "You never cease to astound me."

That evening, after the feast was over, Brynjolf surprised her with a kitten.

"I know I should have given you one after our hand-fasting, but I wanted to get you the perfect one..."

"Awe... I love him. He's so cute." Putting a small dish of cream on a chair for the kitten, she gave Brynjolf his Yule gift.

A new Thor's hammer and a new cloak pin; both made from silver with red jewels decorating the cloak pin.

Taking off his old Thor's hammer he put it on the fireplace before putting on his new one.

The kitten, who she was still thinking of a name for, jumped up on the fireplace to start batting at the Thor's hammer.

Picking up the kitten, she sighed. '*Loki...*' entered her mind and she shook her head.

"No... I'm not naming you Loki."

Brynjolf looked at her.

"Sorry... I feel like I hear things in the back of my head sometimes... I know that that sounds odd or even crazy..."

He smiled and shook his head. "No, it doesn't sound crazy... You have a good relationship with our gods and your ancestors. We're in your ancestral home, so naturally, it's going to happen. You're not crazy for that."

She smiled and kissed him softly. "I'm glad that you don't think I'm crazy... But I'm not naming that cat Loki... No matter how much he wants me to."

He chuckled and shook his head. "You name him whatever you wish to, my love."

She thought about it momentarily as the kitten jumped back up into the chair to drink the cream. "Sigurd... That's what I will name him."

Brynjolf nodded. "A good name for him."

A few months went by and the village began to plant new crops and celebrate the new year coming.

Ostara and Walpurgis were right around the corner with Midsummer not far behind that.

Ostara hit and Adania was working hard on the festival arrangements while Brynjolf was working on things that needed to be done for the clan.

This festival was going to be different from what she was used to. She and Brynjolf decided to combine the traditions of both their clans and make it one large festival.

A large pole stood outside the longhouse with ribbons and garlands of flowers around it. Flower garlands were hung inside the longhouse and throughout the village.

A large bonfire was set up in the training grounds.

Children's activities included making dolls out of twigs and scraps of fabric to throw into a bonfire to ward off evil spirits as was tradition for Dragon clan.

Adania made sure that there was still archery, drinking, dancing, and even included sparring in a small area away from the training grounds.

She decided she would dance around the pole of ribbons and flowers that year.

One of the girls, about six or seven, had Adania bend down and she put a wreath of ribbons and flowers on Adania's head.

Growing up, she had heard stories about how women that wanted children would end up pregnant during that year if they danced around the pole. Adania wasn't so sure how true it was but the older women swore it was as if the pole was blessed by Freyja.

Walpurgis followed after Ostara. This festival was handled by Brynjolf and Adania took over his Jarl duties so that he could plan the festival. A celebration of darkness and revelry.

Large bonfires were lit when the moon was highest in the sky. Children would gather branches and twigs at twilight which were used to decorate the houses within the village. Songs were sung about Odin's sacrifice upon the tree of Yggdrasil to gain the knowledge of the runes and they celebrated this way for nine nights.

Then came Midsummer, a festival of power and activity because the sun was at its highest peak.

Bonfires, which seemed to be a major theme for the born dragon that Adania married.

Model longboats were made by children and then filled with flammable offerings were thrown into the bonfires for Baldur.

Dancing and games are what Adania was used to for Midsummer. Though the dancing was more of a fertility ritual for those that wanted children.

This was also when they would plant their crops for the coming winter.

Chapter 12

Humor

"To learn to find humor in all things."

Adania sat on the bed as she stripped off her shoes, her socks, and her apron dress. Putting her brooches and treasure necklaces down where she normally put them, she laid back on the bed and sighed.

"Today seemed so long..." She closed her eyes momentarily.

Brynjolf walked over to her and began rubbing on her legs, wearing only his pants. "The days do get longer this time of year and you have been working almost non-stop to make sure this festival goes off without issue."

She moaned softly at his touch and moved her foot to caress his thigh. Pulling him towards her, she smiled.

He groaned and looked up at her. "You are treading dangerous territory, Elska."

"Hearing your voice and the sounds you make... makes me want you all the more." She grinned and pulled him to the bed so she could straddle him.

Brynjolf grinned wolfishly as she pinned him to the bed and began rocking her hips against him to tease. He sat up and bit her bottom lip before kissing her soundly and rolling his hips against hers. He murmured against her lips, "You going to ride me tonight, Addy?"

"Perhaps... or I might just tease you to the point you can't stand it." She grinned and shifted to kiss down his neck and then his chest.

Biting softly at the skin of his pectorals, she spoke softly. "Watching you work the last couple of weeks..." she trailed off.

She smirked looking up at him from his stomach before she bit leaving a bright purple hickey against his skin.

He bit his lip and arched into her mouth as she left the hickey on his skin. He sat up slightly and ran his hands through her hair, to see her deep green eyes.

Truthfully, he would give this woman the world if she asked for it.

He pulled her to straddle his hips once more after adjusting his pants. He slid deep into her core with a single stroke.

He rolled his hips into her and growled, "fuck me."

Adania moaned loudly as she tipped her head back. "Fuck..." she leaned forward putting her hands on his chest as she started to grind her hips against his. Her walls tightened around his cock.

She let out a wolf-like growl and grinned. Her nails dug into his chest as she started to grind harder against him before leaning back and putting her hands on his thighs as she started to bounce along his cock.

Brynjolf growled as he watched her roll her body against his, her breasts swaying as she bounced up and down on his length.

He sat up slightly and captured her nipple into his mouth, sucking it to a peak before alternating to the other. He bit down and flicked his tongue back and forth over the nub.

Adania brought a hand to the back of his head to keep him against her nipple. "Fuck, don't stop." She stopped bouncing along his length and started grinding against him again as she tightened against his cock.

Rocking her hips against his, her body tensed. Gripping tightly in his hair as she rolled her hips violently against his. Her walls tightened once more and then spasmed.

Panting heavily, she leaned against him.

Brynjolf grinned and held her close as he released deep into her body. He kissed her neck as his cock pulsed within her core.

She moaned and then collapsed against the bed. "Gods... fuck..." she looked up at the ceiling.

He chuckled as she collapsed next to him.

He brushed his hand along her body and kissed her neck slowly.

She blushed and curled up beside him. "You need to moan more." She grinned looking up at him. "I like the sounds you make." She grinned and kissed him softly.

Brynjolf breathed in slowly as they both began to relax. He kissed along her neck again and bit down playfully.

His lips were soft and feather light across her skin as his fingers caressed down her chest and stomach to the edge of her under-dress. He worked the fabric up and nipped her earlobe.

Throwing the heap of fabric to the floor along with his pants, his fingers softly worked over the nub of her clit.

Adania's breath hitched. Putting a hand on his cheek, she kissed him deeply.

Brynjolf smiled and kissed her back. His thumb slowly brushed over her clit as he nibbled her lip with a growl.

He kissed down her body and sucked a nipple to a peak. His tongue flicking back and forth over the point as his index finger slid into her already wet core

Adania squirmed slightly. Moaning softly, she closed her eyes. Her hips rolled upward against his hand wanting more.

Brynjolf chuckled and licked along his lover's chest, sucking the nipple back into his mouth. His free hand gently tweaked and plucked the other to a point.

He growled against her chest and looked up at her face with a smile.

Her hips rolled upward to meet his hand again. "Bryn..." she whispered his name and pulled him to her kissing him deeply.

Nuzzling his cheek, she moved to straddle him.

Grinding against his groin, she grinned.

Brynjolf groaned and held her hips, rocking his hips upward just enough to tease her.

He sat up and kissed her mouth lovingly. His teeth grazed her lip slowly. Rolling his hips into hers, he rolled her to her back. He gently angled his hips, the tip of his cock teasing her core with each slow rock of his torso.

"I love you Addy... so fucking much." More than he ever thought he would.

Adania groaned wanting more. "Brynjolf…" she pouted. Giggling she pulled him to her and smiled. Wrapping her legs around him she pulled him closer; moaning softly feeling his cock rub against her. "Don't make me fuck you." She teased. "I got no qualms about it. I will ride your cock until day breaks if I have to. Though you have a lot to do tomorrow, right?"

Brynjolf growled and nipped her earlobe with a chuckle, "I have meetings tomorrow, yes. But those things, are not important."

He slid himself slowly but deeply into her core. His eyes rolled back at the feeling of her body. He began a slowly torturous rhythm, "you are my priority right now." His left hand tangled with her right as he kissed down her chest to tease her nipples into peaks again.

Adania moaned loudly and arched upward against him.

She looked up at him and smiled. Squeezing his hand, she kissed him deeply.

Her hand dug into his arm as he thrust slowly. "There are times you're a bastard." She teased. Giggling she rolled her hips against his. "More…" she whined softly.

Brynjolf chuckled and growled on the skin of her breasts. His eyes darkened as he stopped moving altogether, "Oh, I'm fully aware of just how much of a bastard I can be."

He smirked and started at a little bit of a faster pace. His teeth scraped the skin of her breasts again.

"Bryn…" She whispered softly.

Brynjolf growled at the sweet whisper of his name. The way her body wrapped around him in more ways than one. His hips grinding into hers as she rocked up into his, "good girl."

Adania groaned at the sound of his voice. The way it danced across her skin. The deep throaty sound of it as it left his mouth.

"Bryn…" she whispered again. The way his mouth felt against her skin made her whole body tighten. Moaning loudly, she rolled her hips in time with his.

Brynjolf smiled at the eager way she surrendered herself to him. The way she arched and moaned for more.

More of his touch.

His cock.

His words.

He growled low next to her ear and nipped the lobe, "yes, Elska?"

Adania panted looking up at him and smiled.

Kissing him deeply she rolled her hips against his. "I love the feel of you…" she groaned and nibbled on his neck before leaving a hickey there.

"I love you… so much." She whispered putting her forehead against his.

Brynjolf growled softly and chuckled as she whispered her adoration into his mouth.

Their kisses became more feverish as they continued. He panted and bit her lip softly, "I love you too."

Her hips rolled against his more. "Please." She grinned.

He held off on his own orgasm and reached down to stroke her clit with his thumb.

Her breath hitched against his mouth at the touch to her clit. "Cheat."

Brynjolf laughed evilly at her exclamation that he was a cheat. He groaned into her mouth and continued to stroke her clit as she rolled her hips faster. He growled and nibbled her lip.

He sucked in his breath as his cock began tingling at the tip. "Fuck, I'm so close."

He bit her shoulder as he came, his body bucking into hers making him groan softly as she came right along with him.

He gently slid himself from her.

Chuckling, he moved his mouth to the shell of her ear. He groaned slowly and smirked, "Adania, I love you. We should get some rest."

Nodding, she smiled up at him. "Fine." She pouted and kissed him.

Rolling herself over she put her back against his chest and her ass up against his crotch as she started to relax against him.

Brynjolf yawned and nuzzled her neck as she relaxed into his chest, his arms locked securely around her. He kissed her shoulder and slowly settled off to sleep with her at his side.

As Adania slept, she had a dream.

This one was different from the ones she had had about Brynjolf.

Here she was, standing around what she thought were the roots of Yggdrasil looking around.

The well of Urdr's water was a crystalline blue as she looked within it.

Three women stepped out from the shadows.

"The Norn?" She blinked a few times and bowed her head in respect to the three that guarded the fate of all in Midgard and Asgard.

One of them spoke. Her voice was somewhat raspy but ethereal. "I am Urdr. Welcome to the well, young one."

Another stepped forward, her voice ethereal but not raspy like the first. She sounded young and full of energy. "I am Verdandi. We are here to guide you, Adania."

The third stepped forward this time. She was holding something. Her voice ethereal as well but also childlike. "I am Skuld. The gift I hold is for you." She smiled and handed the wrapping to Adania.

A small baby slept within the wrappings.

Skuld gave a giggle and moved back toward the well.

Urdr spoke again. "She is yours and the dragon's. A gift from Freyja to have us give to you. Take care young wolf. She will be much more like you and Brynjolf than you will care to admit.

Verdandi smiled and waved at Adania. "Our time is short, but we will help you along the way."

Adania awoke with a groan. Instinctively, she put her hand on her belly. "I'm going to have a baby?" She said to herself. Brynjolf was downstairs making breakfast. Had she really slept that long? Looking around for her under-dress and socks, the sun stung her eyes as it shone through the window. She cursed to herself at how bright it was.

Groaning, she got dressed and went downstairs. Yawning she stretched. "Morning Bryn..." She sighed.

"Morning Elska... Are you alright? You were tossing and turning pretty badly last night."

"I'm fine my love." She smiled and kissed his cheek as she went over to grab food. "Just a dream I had last night."

He looked at her. "Do you want to talk about it?"

Sitting down, she sighed again.

Getting up the courage to tell him about it, as well as her own interpretation of it, she told him as she ate.

He blinked a few times. "Does this mean we're going to have a baby?"

She shrugged. "I don't know. That would be my assumption considering the Norn look after the fate of everything... Skuld kept saying she... Does that mean we're going to have a girl then?"

Brynjolf grinned and went over to Adania. Kissing her softly, he put a hand on her cheek. "Whether boy or girl. As long as it's healthy and you are healthy. That's all that matters to me."

Adania smiled up at him. "You say that now until she brings home her first boyfriend." She teased.

His face flashed a bit of worry, anger, and sadness almost all at the same time before he sighed, "Have you ever thought of names?"

Adania swallowed a mouthful of bacon and eggs. "I never thought I would have a husband; let alone children. Though if it is a girl and if you are alright with it… I want to name her Runa."

Brynjolf nodded. "That's perfectly fine with me, Addy… Though, she's going to have a lot to live up to giving her such a name."

Adania nodded. "I know… but if we are going to have a baby… I guess that pole really is legendary for women having children after touching it." She laughed some then and shrugged.

He chuckled and kissed her forehead. "I guess we both shouldn't have touched it." He winked and laughed as she hit his chest.

"I blame you."

"As I recall, you weren't complaining last night… or any other night for that matter."

Her face went a bright shade of pink. "That's not the point, Brynjolf."

He grinned and cleaned up the dishes. "I want you to go easy on everything for a while. Alright? I have other Jarls to talk to today. Why don't you go see Randvi and talk to her about it? I'll have Ulfric watch over training for the time being."

"Brynjolf… We don't even know if I am or not."

"I just want you to be careful, just in case."

Now she knew how Runa felt when Runa had been pregnant. "Fine… Though I still intend to keep working and doing things."

He sighed. "Stubborn wolf."

"Damned dragon."

CHAPTER 13

TRUTH

"To tell the truth in every situation is always the best course of action. Anything else is to be a coward."

Hillevi had been trying to get close to Adania and Adania wanted nothing to do with her. Especially now that she was, in fact, pregnant.

The woman was constantly trying to get Adania to fight with Brynjolf or get him to fight with her, and much to her dismay, it hadn't worked.

Adania was fed up with it.

One morning, while Brynjolf and many of the men were working on the longhouse and adding in rooms for Gunnar and the baby, Adania was out shopping in the marketplace to get ingredients for dinner, as well as some thread and fabric to make a blanket for both children.

She came across Hillevi. In public, she was sickeningly sweet, but once no one was around, she turned into the most vile woman.

Naturally, Adania was nice in public. She had to be. She was Jarlskona and she didn't want to cause a problem for Brynjolf either.

Today was going to be the day. She had a bad feeling about it.

Hillevi made a comment to Adania about Brynjolf eventually getting bored with her and he would come crawling back to her.

Adania lost it. "What the fuck is your problem with me? You've been giving me bullshit since Brynjolf and I had our hand-fasting... And pregnant or not, I have no problem kicking your ass."

"Brynjolf was supposed to take me as his wife. Then he comes here to raid and instantly takes you... You used some kind of wolf clan magic on him, didn't you?"

Adania raised an eyebrow at the woman. "So, you're jealous that the man you had feelings for ended up with me instead of you?"

"This isn't mere jealousy... He promised I would be his Jarlskona and we would have kids together... I had him in my bed countless times."

"And If I ask Brynjolf about this, will he tell me the same?"

Hillevi looked taken aback by this and stammered as she tried to speak.

Adania held up a hand to cut her off before she spoke, "I'm not going to just take you at your word. You've been trying to cause problems with Brynjolf and I since our hand-fasting. Let's go talk to Brynjolf then, shall we?"

Hillevi composed herself. "If you think you need to talk to him about this then go ahead."

"Oh no... You're coming with me. I will drag you up to the longhouse by your hair if I have to."

The two made it to the longhouse, arguing the entire time.

"Brynjolf!" Adania yelled up to him as they topped the hill.

Hillevi ran up to him making herself cry. "Brynjolf... Adania said horrible, mean things to me today. I think it's the pregnancy getting to her." She went to throw her arms around him and he pushed her away with a sigh.

"Adania, I told you I would go to the marketplace today to get everything. You should rest."

Adania shook her head. "I can't sit around all day. Besides the walking makes me feel better."

He sighed. "Fine, I know better than to argue with you by now." He kissed her forehead. "So, what is this about?" He gestured over to Hillevi.

Adania told him everything that happened from the hand-fasting up until they crested the hill, Hillevi trying to interject herself every chance she got.

"She's lying... I have been nothing but nice to her."

Brynjolf had had enough.

He growled and looked at Hillevi. "Do you know what the punishment is for insulting my wife?"

Hillevi stopped and looked at him. "But she's lying, she's trying to take you away from me... We were supposed to-"

Brynjolf stopped her. "She never took me from you. You did that yourself. I never promised you any of the things you have told her, nor have we been in bed together."

Hillevi looked like she was about to cry again.

Adania folded her arms across her chest.

He turned to Hillevi and looked at her. "I'm banishing you from Dragon clan... You insult me, my wife, this clan. I'm tired of the lying and the underhanded *bullshit* you do. I should have done this a long time ago... Everything you own is stripped from you. If you return here then I will let Adania have the pleasure of ending your life. You are no longer welcome here."

"Brynjolf..." She whined.

"No. Enough. Leave."

Hillevi looked at him. "You'll regret this Brynjolf." She spat and left without so much as another word.

Her words made Adania's blood run cold. There was truth to them. She would make him regret the banishment but when or how was another story.

Adania sighed and looked at Brynjolf. "I'm sorry that you had to do such a thing."

Brynjolf shook his head. "Don't be. It should have been done a long time ago, I was the coward for not doing it sooner and you have suffered for it."

Adania put a hand on his cheek. "Bryn... You are no coward... At times controlling and sometimes insatiable... but never a coward. You are one of the most honorable men I know."

He smiled at her and took her hand from his face. "I have a few things to finish up in Gunnar's room and then I will come and help you with dinner."

Adania rolled her eyes and put her hands on her hips. "I'm pregnant, not an invalid... but I won't turn down the help."

Brynjolf chuckled and nodded. "Alright. Forgive me for worrying about you and our child."

She kissed him and went to go work on dinner.

True to his word, he came in some time later covered in sweat and dirt.

"You're not helping while you're still filthy." Adania scolded.

He grabbed a piece of bread from the table and snickered some as she scolded him the entire time.

"Don't be like a pig and eat while you're covered in filth... That's disgusting."

"I love you too Addy. I'll clean up and I'll be in to help."

"I'm almost done actually, so go clean up."

Brynjolf came back in after washing himself. He was in fresh clothes and smelled of soap.

"Are you going to tell me the history you have with Hillevi?" Adania asked as she set the table.

Brynjolf took the plates from her and sighed. "I guess I should... We promised each other no secrets."

"I don't want it to be an issue..."

He shook his head. "It's not Addy... She and I grew up together in Dragon clan. Her father was really close to mine. She kept chasing after men with station and wealth, particularly the warriors. That's all she ever wanted. She used people to get the things she has. She's almost never been told no and throws a tantrum when she doesn't get her way... Most men wanted nothing to do with her once they found out she was just after them for their money or a title. I was nice to her because of our fathers. I swear though, I never slept with her and I never promised to make her my wife."

Adania smiled at him. "I don't doubt you Brynjolf. Plus, you're a terrible liar. You never look at me when you try to lie."

He blinked at her a few times and grinned. "You're a terrible liar too."

She hit his arm playfully and shrugged. "My father always told me that to tell anything but the truth is to be a coward. So, I never learned to lie."

"I guess that works out for me then." He smirked.

"Ass." she teased and kissed his cheek.

The two ate dinner, joked, and laughed.

Once dinner was over, Adania grabbed some fabric and started to try and work on doing some embroidery for the baby.

She was trying to make a dress with wolves and dragons on it.

Brynjolf looked at her and smiled as he watched her. "Your embroidery has gotten a lot better as of late."

Looking up from the fabric, she sighed. "I don't feel like it. I still feel like it looks like shit."

He shook his head. "Elska, it doesn't. I promise. I know you have never really ever been one to do embroidery and I know it's still hard for you to do sometimes and you get frustrated easily with it, but I do enjoy it when you put some on my tunics, your dresses, Gunnar's clothes, and I'm sure eventually Runa's clothes will be decorated by your hands."

"I have much better control over a sword than I do a needle."

He chuckled. "You do. There is a grace to you when you hold a blade versus when you hold a needle, but it still fascinates me that you are able to do such work with the same hands that tried to kill me."

She snickered then. "Sorry about that."

Brynjolf rubbed his jawline. "My jaw still hurts occasionally by the way, but don't be sorry. I wouldn't have wanted you as a wife if you were like every other woman that I've ever met."

"Lucky for me then." She teased and went back to working on the embroidery in her lap.

Brynjolf and several of the other males finished the longhouse additions before the first snow. Gunnar was moved to his own room and Adania was now very pregnant and showing.

She had been visited by the Norn several more times since the additions started and up until the completion, and each time she told Randvi and Brynjolf about her dreams. Quite often she would see a girl with dark brown hair and green eyes, the same green eyes and dark brown hair that Brynjolf had.

Runa looked to be about twelve when she would play by the well and with the Norn when the dreams had stopped.

Chapter 14
Accountability

"You are the only one responsible for your own destiny, your own life, and your own actions."

The Ostara festival was on hold after Adania went into labor. Brynjolf was in the room with her along with Randvi, Revna, and Helga.

Typically, men weren't allowed in the room, but both he and Adania insisted on him being there.

A couple of hours had passed and there was almost no progress. Adania was exhausted and sweaty.

At one point, Revna had to go get Ulfric to peel Brynjolf away from Adania.

Shoving both men out the door, she closed and locked it.

A couple more hours had passed and Brynjolf was pacing up and down the floor of the longhouse. Ulfric sat on a chair with his arms folded across his chest.

"Let the wolves do their magic... things... that they do." His voice was gruff as he watched Brynjolf's pacing.

"That woman better keep my wife and child alive or I'm going to kill her."

Ulfric shook his head. "If Adania is even half as stubborn as you are, she'll be fine. And that baby is half of you so I'm sure it will be fine."

Finally, Revna came out shutting the door behind her.

Brynjolf looked at her waiting for an answer.

"Your daughter and Adania are fine. It was rough but they are safe." Her voice was soft as she spoke.

Brynjolf released the breath he had been holding. "Thank the gods…" he whispered softly.

Ulfric chuckled. "See, I told you she would be fine."

"Adania is severely exhausted and she's resting. You will have to introduce your daughter to the clan once Adania has rested for a little while."

Brynjolf looked at her and nodded. "Can I go in and be with them?"

Revna nodded and opened the door for him. "Just do so quietly or Randvi might try to kill you. Adania has had a lot of herbs and magic to keep her here."

He went through the door and watched as Randvi and Helga were cleaning up everything.

Adania was already trying to get up.

"Wolfling. Sit your ass back down on that bed and rest." Randvi scolded.

Helga sighed and took Runa over to Brynjolf to hold, mainly so that she could help the older woman with a very stubborn Jarlskona.

Brynjolf looked down at the baby and smiled. Going over to the bed, he sat down and looked at Adania. "Addy, lay down and rest. You just had a baby… our baby. I will go introduce her to the clan so that you can rest. You need it. You have been at this for hours."

Adania looked up at him panting. "I'm fine… And I want to be there when you introduce her to everyone."

"Elska…" He smiled at her and put his forehead against hers. "I almost lost you. I'm not going to let you be reckless and end up hurting yourself."

She groaned and closed her eyes. "Fine… but I'm not going to be happy about it."

He chuckled as Adania sat back against the head of the bed.

"Runa Brynjolfdottir is going to be a mouthful for everyone." Adania smiled up at him.

"I'm sure she will earn a name at some point... Most do." He looked down at his daughter as he spoke.

"How did you get Drekkin anyway? I kept forgetting to ask..."

Brynjolf looked up at her. "I never told you the story on that?"

Adania shook her head.

He sighed and put Runa in the bed he had made for her as she yawned. "At one point, I had taken bacon grease into my mouth, grabbed a torch, and spit the grease toward several men that thought they could raid my home. My father had died the winter before and I was a young Jarl then. Most of the other clans tried to raid my home thinking that because I was so young that I was weak. They found out the hard way... Fire is very heavy in our traditions, as you have seen. It was just after my thirteenth winter. The raiding party didn't see me grab the jar of grease. They only saw me spitting fire. Naturally, that's when the stories started and I was then being called 'the dragon' rather than Hranison."

Adania watched him as he told the story. Snickering to herself, she shook her head. "I don't think bacon grease would taste very good."

He laughed some and looked at her. "No... No, it didn't but I was young and that was the first thing I thought of to fend off the invaders. As the story spread, raids slowly dwindled to nothing." He shrugged. "I guess it worked wonders on my reputation."

"Honestly, I hadn't heard anything about it, but we're also pretty far removed from most of the other clans."

"You also didn't recognize me when I came to your shores."

She cocked her head to the side and looked at him with a puzzled expression. "What do you mean? We met before the raid?"

Shaking his head, he gave his half-cocked smirk that she adored. "We met back when we were kids. The Althing. It was the first time you had ever seen flyting."

How had I not realized that before?

"Is my memory really that bad?" She sighed.

Brynjolf kissed her forehead. "I blame that fact of your training. You got hit in the head too many times."

"Hey!" Punching his arm playfully she looked at him. "If it wasn't for the fact that I just went hours of pushing our daughter out of my body I would be kicking your ass right now."

"Elska. I love you… I really do… But I don't think you can. You haven't been able to do it any time that we have done training together."

Randvi had the other two take her herbs and tools back to the hut. "Jarl. Jarlskona. I hate to interrupt. However, there are a few things you will need to do and several things you can't do after just having a baby."

"Oh?" Adania looked at the woman not realizing she had still been in the room.

"No sex for the next couple of weeks. It can cause bleeding and I really don't want to have to smack my Jarl around for being too rough."

Brynjolf groaned, "Fine. I'm not that rough with her anyway."

She looked at him. "When the entire village can hear you two. I'd say you're being too rough."

Adania blushed a deep scarlet.

Randvi looked at the couple. "You're not allowed to pick up anything heavier than the baby. We don't want you to end up hurting yourself. You will also have to present the baby to the clan. I don't want you standing for too long and I don't want you sitting for too long either. I'll send Revna and Helga over every day to check on you, and to make sure that you both are doing okay. If you need a break at night, I can always have them come by and help out."

"Thank you Randvi. I will try not to do too much, though I can't promise anything."

Randvi flicked the woman on the nose. "You will do what you are supposed to do wolfling or else."

Adania rubbed her nose. "Damned old woman."

"Stubborn whelp." She sighed. "But I will check on you from time to time and make sure you are healing properly." Randvi handed a small bag of herbs to Adania. "These will help with the pain. Do not take more than a pinch at a time. Try to space it out every couple of hours. You can put them in tea or just chew on them… Now, with tradition. What are you going to be naming her?"

Brynjolf looked at the old woman then. "Runa."

Randvi smiled and took a small cup of water. Dipping her fingers into it, she sprinkled Runa with the water and wrote small runes on her forehead and feet. "Welcome to the clan, Runa Drekkindottir."

Adania looked at Brynjolf. "Looks like Randvi gave her a fitting name. Daughter of the Dragon. I feel sorry for anyone that decides to try and date her once she's older."

The look on Brynjolf's face made Adania shudder and laugh all at the same time.

Randvi turned back to look at the couple. "Alright. I am going to be heading back to my hut. If you need me, come get me."

Adania nodded. "Of course. Thank you again, Randvi."

Randvi went out to update everyone that Adania was fine and that she and Brynjolf had had a daughter. She announced that Brynjolf and Adania would introduce the baby to the clan once Adania had had enough rest.

Adania heard the yelling and cheering from her and Brynjolf's room, making her snicker.

"Once those herbs wear off a bit I want to walk around, and take Runa out to meet everyone... Also... It's tradition here that you introduce her and officially announce her name, but that is entirely up to you if you want to keep that tradition or not..."

He nodded. "I think we should keep it, but I don't want you pushing yourself. You really should take it easy at least for the next several days... I know that's not going to happen. You are by far the most stubborn woman I know."

"You wouldn't have me any other way. Besides, you married me. It's your fault that I'm stubborn." She teased.

"I highly doubt it's my fault. I heard stories about you when you were a child from Randvi and a few of the others. You were stubborn even as a child."

She shrugged then. "I blame my upbringing."

He kissed her forehead. "Do you need me to bring you anything? Water? Food?"

She looked up at him and smiled as she touched his cheek. The stubble on his cheeks grazed against her skin. "Water, food, and fresh clothes would be nice."

"I will help you into your dress. Don't argue with me on it either."

She shook her head. "Hadn't planned on it. Despite the herbs that Randvi filled my body with, I'm still in some pain, but it's manageable." She shrugged.

"They aren't meant to take it away completely. Just meant to make it tolerable."

"I know, but still."

"What colors do you want to wear?"

"Doesn't matter to me, Brynjolf. Why not something that matches your clothes?"

He nodded. "Will do. Don't move from that bed or else."

She smiled at him. "I won't move. Promise."

"Good girl." he teased and left to go get her the things she had asked for.

Coming back a little while later with a plate in one hand of bread, some cheese, butter, and apples, a large drinking horn full of water in the other hand, and her clothes thrown over his shoulder.

His tunic was a light blue with accents in green. The under-dress he grabbed for her was a shade of dark green while her apron dress was blue.

She and Astrid had made several sets of matching clothes for her and Brynjolf. Though they didn't wear matching clothes most of the time, Adania figured it would be a nice thing to do for festivals and important occasions.

Adania and Brynjolf sat together on the bed and talked as she ate on the food he had brought for her.

Once she was feeling up to move around, she got up, and with his help, and changed into the clothes he had brought for her.

He wasn't happy about her moving around too much, but she promised she would sit down through most of the festival and only move when she needed to. Of course, he still wasn't happy about it, but he relented.

"I know once your mind is made up there's no use trying to change it."

"No, not normally."

He picked up the baby and held her, still amazed that she was his daughter. "Let's go officially introduce her."

Adania nodded, "I'm sure everyone wants to see her."

The couple walked out of the longhouse. Adania stopping periodically to catch her breath. She hadn't realized how hard it was going to be to do simple tasks for the next few days.

Brynjolf walked forward a few steps from Adania after making sure she was steady and she could stand on her own.

"Everyone… I would like all of you to meet the newest dragon. Her name is Runa."

The ones that gathered around cheered once again.

Astrid came up and handed Adania some red linen. "There is enough there to make you and Runa a dress. I'm happy for you, Adania. If you or Brynjolf need anything let me know. I can even watch Runa for you if you need a break."

Adania hugged her and smiled. "Thank you, Astrid. It means a lot to me."

Brynjolf handed Runa to Adania and grabbed the fabric to take it back to the longhouse.

There was no way she was going to make that walk all the way back to their room alone. Plus… Brynjolf would most likely not allow her to do it on her own anyway.

This was the one of the few times she decided she wasn't going to sass him about it.

Runa yawned and opened her eyes enough to look around. Her eyes went to the large tree.

Her eyes were a deep green like her mother's, rather than her father's like Adania had dreamt about.

Brynjolf came back not long after he put the fabric away. "Shall we go ahead and celebrate today?"

Adania nodded and smiled. "I won't be drinking, but I will indulge in food and other activities."

Brynjolf smiled at his wife. "Just don't overdo it."

She rolled her eyes at him. "I'll be fine. I'm not going to be doing much. I might stand and do some archery or throw axes, but otherwise, I'm not going to be standing a whole lot. I'm still in a decent amount of pain and I know if I push too much, I'm going to end up in more pain… And no thank you. I'm good."

Brynjolf grinned. "Good. Glad you learned your lesson." He teased and took Runa from her. He walked with Adania over to the festival grounds where the archery and thrown weapons were. She participated and did fairly well, even in pain.

Brynjolf participated in some of the fighting and drinking, and he too did fairly well in both.

He much preferred the juniper and raspberry mead that had been made by Yrsa compared to the hand-to-hand combat.

Adania took Runa up to the tree and touched it. Sighing, she put a cup of mead down at the roots and began to talk. "Hello, dad. Runa. Gunnar... I wanted you to meet the newest member of the family. We named her Runa. I hope that you all will protect her. I miss all of you and I really wish that you all would have gotten to meet her. Baby Gunnar is healthy and always getting into things, though he's not much of a baby anymore. He is much like his parents and very much does not like when we tell him no... I need to get back to my husband and Gunnar, but I wanted to make sure that you all were included in the festival too. So, I will let you all get back to whatever it is that you were doing."

The wind blew softly and she thought she heard her father's voice saying, '*thank you*', which made her smile.

Taking Runa back over to Brynjolf, she smiled. "Let's go ahead and settle down for the evening. The kids need to sleep and I'm pretty tired myself."

CHAPTER 15
SELF-RELIANCE

"To provide everything needed without outside help."

Adania yet again found herself visited by the Norn. Another baby was given to her. The middle sister seemed excited about handing her the second baby.

"He's going to be a handful little wolfling." She giggled.

Adania smiled. "Well, looks like I have to go tell Brynjolf again."

The oldest of the Norn nodded. "This will also be the last time that you visit the well."

Adania cocked her head to the side. "I won't have anymore?"

The old woman shook her head. "No, but you have done well and will do well with the ones you have, dear child."

Adania nodded. "I am happy that the gods have bestowed two upon me and Brynjolf."

"It will be rough but you will be fine."

Adania awoke to the sun creeping into the room. She heard the two kids and Brynjolf within the longhouse. Grabbing her coat, she went to go get breakfast.

Brynjolf was playing with Gunnar and Runa. It was winter and the snow coated the ground like a blanket.

"Runa, Gunnar. We have some training to do today."

"More?" Gunnar complained.

"Yes. More." Adania snickered.

Brynjolf walked over to Adania and kissed her softly.

"Eww... Gross." Gunnar stuck his tongue out at the two.

Adania laughed and smiled up at Brynjolf. "I was visited by the Norn again."

"Really?" He smiled and kissed her forehead this time. "What about this time?"

"Apparently, we are going to have a son this time."

"As long as you both are healthy. That's all that matters to me... Just try not to scare me like you did when Runa was born. I don't think I could handle losing you."

Adania smiled at him and kissed his cheek. "You'll get to be a father for the third time."

He grinned at her and nodded. "Just as you get to be a mother again."

They both laughed some and then went on with the day ahead.

Runa helped around the longhouse doing chores and Gunnar helped Brynjolf with outside work.

Several months later, Adania was holding a baby boy wrapped in a blanket. "What shall we name him Bryn?"

Adania looked up at him and smiled, her face covered in sweat.

"What about Eilif?"

She nodded. "Sounds good to me."

"I love you, Addy. I will present him to the clan later this evening. I have some other things to attend to today.

"Oh? What's going on?" She started to sit up.

He sighed. "I didn't want to stress you about it, but it seems that Raven clan calls for aid. They have been attacked over the last several weeks. I don't know what to do for them."

Adania sighed and took his hand. "Raven clan is among our closest allies... at least when it was just Wolf clan. Which means they are your allies too, as well as Serpent and Bear."

He nodded. "Then help them we will... I will deal with it. You rest."

"Like Hel, I will."

He sighed. "Addy, my love. Please, you just had our second child. I'm sure Randvi will tell you the same thing she told you a few years ago. That you need to rest and relax."

Randvi sighed as she put her things away, "He's right wolfling. Nothing heavier than the baby. No sex. I'm sure you remember everything I told you." She scowled at the redhead.

She groaned. "I'm fine. I need to get up and walk around anyway."

"Addy, you just had a baby." Brynjolf pinched the bridge of his nose and sighed.

"And?"

"You stubborn wolf."

She smiled up at him then.

Within a few days, Adania was up and walking around with Eilif.

Sitting next to Brynjolf in the longhouse, she listened to the Jarl and Jarlskona of Raven clan talk about the clan that raided them and burned their entire home to the ground.

The description of the woman made Adania sit up straight as she looked at Brynjolf, and he looked back at her.

"There's no way in Helheim..." He spoke softly.

"She said she would make you regret banishing her Bryn."

"Aye, she did." He sighed and looked at the two standing before him. "We will take your clan in and help where we can. But please try not to upset my people."

"Thank you, Jarl Drekkin."

"Just Brynjolf is fine. I will do what I can where I can, as will Adania."

Adania smiled and nodded at the two.

"They have the banner of the Boar. They never used to be a violent clan but ever since their new Jarl took over... He turned them into nothing more than brutes... and then add that wretch of a woman... They have been trying to expand their own territory... Anyone that doesn't join them they banish or downright kill them." The woman spoke. "It's terrifying... I would expect such things from Bear clan, not Boar..."

Adania thought for a moment. "What colors does Boar clan use?" The words left her mouth before she even processed the thought. "black and yellow." The woman responded and looked at Adania.

"Black and yellow…" Adania thought for a moment again. "I've seen that before… Damn it… Where… Ugh. I wish my memory wasn't as shitty as it is." She sighed.

"Addy?" Brynjolf looked at her. "What it is?"

"I remember seeing black and yellow on longboats before but I can't remember where… I'm sure Odin will give me some insight into it later… He always does."

The couple in front of them smiled. "You two have come a long way since we first heard about the union of Wolf and Dragon clans." The woman snickered some. "We're glad that we still have an ally though."

The male spoke then. "Forgive me. I didn't introduce myself or my wife… I am Brynjar Erlandson and this is my wife, Sylvi Thorgarddottir."

Adania stood up and smiled at them. Bowing her head slightly. "It is an honor to meet you both, and it is an honor to help you in your times of need."

Brynjolf stood with Adania putting an arm around her back. "You both are more than welcome to stay here in the longhouse with us. There are a few houses that we have built as guest houses though I don't know how many clansmen you have brought with you."

"There's about fifty or so of us that managed to leave with us."

"We have enough houses for that many people. Each house has a few bedrooms. Though they might have to share houses until this all gets sorted out." Adania spoke softly.

Brynjar nodded. "That's fine. It's a roof, which is better than nothing."

"Things are going to be strained for a little while but we will make it through and we will help you with resources as best as we can."

"Thank you… both of you. We appreciate everything you can do." Sylvi spoke and smiled at them.

"I will have Hrafn send a message to Serpent and Bear to see if they can aid as well. I don't know how much they can do but we will see what we can muster. Anything will help right now."

Brynjolf grinned as he looked at Adania before kissing the side of her head. "And you said you don't like dealing in politics." He whispered so only she could hear. "I'm proud of you."

She shrugged and handed him Eilif. "I will return after I go speak with our bird master." With that, she left to go speak to Hrafn about getting messages to Bear and Serpent clans. She didn't doubt that Serpent would answer the call for aid, though she wasn't so sure about Bear.

She knew that by asking for help that she was going against her father's teachings on providing everything without help, but he would have to forgive her. This problem was far more than she and Brynjolf could handle alone... Especially with having an infant.

"Sorry daddy..." she whispered to herself and continued to walk toward Hrafn's hut to send the letters.

Hrafn gladly got his two most reliable birds to send the messages. Two ravens.

She prayed silently to Odin that the message got to Jerrick at the very least. Sending two ravens was a healthy omen, right?

Once it was done, she headed back up to the longhouse. "I sent word to Serpent and Bear. I'm sure that Jerrick of Serpent clan will answer the call for aid. I'm not so sure about Bear clan. I haven't seen Gudbrand in a few years... The Althing before Runa was born was the last time I saw him." She shrugged. "And Runa will have her fourth winter this year."

Everyone was getting along for the first several weeks, then that's when everything started to strain.

Jerrick had answered the call to help and brought longships of resources from his own territory. Furs, food, and wood.

Jerrick hugged Adania and looked at Brynjolf. "So, this is the mighty dragon that tamed the wild wolf. Doesn't seem that impressive." He smirked and looked at Adania.

Adania shook her head. "What am I going to do with you Jerrick?" She smiled. "Jerrick, this is my husband, Brynjolf. Bryn, this is Jerrick. You two play nice alright?"

Brynjolf looked at Jerrick and stuck his arm out. "Adania speaks highly of Serpent clan. I hope that we will be as good of friends as she is with your clan."

"She's definitely something Brynjolf. You're a lucky man." Jerrick took Brynjolf's arm and they pulled each other into a hug.

"Thanks, Jerrick. And, of course, anytime you need us, don't hesitate to ask for help."

"Thank you, Dragon." Jerrick teased and smiled up at him. "Though I can't stay long this time. I wish I could so that I could help out more than what I have brought. Ivar is looking after my clan until I can return. I wanted to make sure that you got what we brought and that my longships didn't get filled with nothing but Wolf clan mead for the trip home."

He stayed for a couple of days and then left to go back to his own home to prepare his clan for an invasion from Boar clan. Should it happen.

Things at Dragon clan were now going as smoothly as falling on a rock.

Tensions were high, and Adania and Brynjolf were stressed and agitated.

Everyone in the clans were stressed. It was wreaking havoc.

Adania spoke to Brynjolf often about the situation and helped with what she could, but with tensions on the verge of snapping. It was rough, to say the least.

Hillevi was on the warpath and her new clan was backing her up on it.

Adania, of course, felt like it was entirely all her fault. "What are we going to do?" she sighed and looked at Brynjolf.

"We'll get through this, Elska." He smiled at her and kissed her forehead gently. He touched his nose to hers. "We've made it this far and you still tolerate my ass."

She snickered and looked up at him. "A nice ass that it is." Adania teased. "Let's go ahead and do what we need to for the day. I'll take the kids with me so that you can focus on your work."

"Alright. As long as you're sure."

"It'll be fine. I feel like I need to teach Gunnar some things should Hillevi show her ugly traitorous face."

"His sword work is coming along nicely. I have seen him practice when we don't have him doing chores."

"He has come a long way, though he still has a lot to learn."

He smiled. "With you teaching him, I'm sure he will pick up on it fairly easily."

"I want to make sure that all of our children can defend themselves should they need too."

He nodded in agreement, "Runa and Gunnar are both learning so quickly and I'm sure that Eilif will be the same."

"Once he's able to hold a weapon, then I will have him learning too."

"With you, myself and Ulfric teaching them… I don't think anyone will be able to stand a chance. And if Runa ends up anything like you then the only one that is going to be able to handle her is a berserker." He grinned.

CHAPTER 16
Cunning

"To think outside the box and not make a mess big enough that you can't get out of."

Adania was with the children one afternoon when she heard the war horns. "Gods damn it..." She growled. "Gunnar, get into the longhouse. Protect Runa and Eilif the best you can until Helga and Revna can get to you."

"I'll do what I can."

"You're a good, strong boy. I have faith in you. Have faith in your own abilities." She smiled and kissed his forehead. Leaving the tannery, she ran with them to the longhouse.

Once they were close to the longhouse she handed Eilif to Gunnar. "Stay safe. Do what you can okay? Helga and Revna will be on the way soon."

"Be safe yourself Adania. May Tyr and Thor protect and guide you." Gunnar spoke as he held Eilif.

Kissing all of them on the forehead once again, she started to run down the hill that the longhouse sat upon toward the shore passing Revna and Helga along the way. "The kids are already at the longhouse. Please look after them."

"Of course, Jarlskona." Helga nodded.

Revna followed suit. "With my life, if I have to."

"Thank you." With that Adania continued running. Going to the blacksmith's, she grabbed a sword and shield that she was able to wield comfortably.

She and Brynjolf met up with one another halfway down to the docks.

"It's the clan of Boar," Brynjolf yelled over the ruckus that was already being made.

"The kids are already at the longhouse with Helga and Revna heading up that way." She yelled as she cut a man down. "They can protect them until we are able to get back up there."

"Just like old times isn't it, Elska?" He grinned as he watched her cut another man down with a slap of the shield and a stabbing with her sword.

"Less talking... More fighting." She scolded him as she panted. *Gods, this is really difficult.*

"*Wolfling... Longhouse...*" Came Randvi's voice from behind Adania as she heard yelling from the same direction, making her look up to see a fire starting on the longhouse.

"Brynjolf!"

"Get the kids! I got this." Brynjolf yelled as he threw a male off of him and ran his blade through the man's stomach.

Adania didn't have to be told twice. She was running back up the hill as quickly as she could to the longhouse while sheathing her blade.

"Mark my words Hillevi. I will kill you myself if harm comes to my kids." She growled as she ran.

Praying to any god that would answer her, she made it back up the hill and right outside the longhouse.

Revna and Helga had Runa and Eilif in hand who were both crying. "Take them to the training grounds. Where's Gunnar?"

"He said he saw someone and went out the back of the longhouse," Revna spoke panicked as she held Eilif.

Adania sighed and kissed Runa and Eilif on the forehead quickly and hoped that it was enough to stop their crying. "I'll come to the training grounds once I find Gunnar."

Revna and Helga left with the two children in tow.

Adania ran through the longhouse covering her mouth and nose with some of the furs she had on. "Gunnar!"

"Adania!"

"Boy, you scared the shit out of me." She ran through the longhouse and out the back coughing as she grabbed his arm pulling him from the longhouse. "Damn, I really liked that longhouse. But you, Runa, and Eilif are far more important..." She coughed some and looked at him. "You alright?"

He nodded. "I saw a woman set fire to the longhouse. I tried to catch her, but I couldn't find her through the smoke."

She sighed and hugged him tightly. "Don't scare me like that again."

"Sorry, Adania."

She kissed his forehead. "Your mom and dad would be so proud of you."

He smiled up at her and she took him to the training grounds where most of the clan that couldn't fight that well already gathered since the longhouse would need to be rebuilt.

"That woman better pray to whatever god she believes in, and I hope they grant her mercy because I fucking won't." Adania hissed under her breath.

Not seeing Brynjolf, she made sure that Gunnar got to Revna and Helga before she went back to where Brynjolf had been fighting.

"Tyr, God of justice. A child of Midgard calls to you. Help me walk into this battle without fear and to walk unwavering through blood and steel. Give me the strength to protect my children, my husband, and my people." She prayed softly as she ran.

A renewed vigor rushed through her body.

Running up where she had been fighting alongside Brynjolf earlier, there was Hillevi, straddling him with a dagger to an already bleeding eye.

Without hesitation, she tackled the woman to the ground.

Getting thrown off the woman, she scrambled to get up. "Great wolf Fenrir. Hear my words and give me strength. Lend me your power. I am a child of the wolf." Adania spoke softly.

"You think your gods will help you?" Hillevi sounded almost hysterical.

"They already have. My children are safe no thanks to you."

Brynjolf propped himself up on a rock trying to gain his bearings as he tried to watch the two women. "Elska..."

Adania didn't even take her eyes off Hillevi. "You have done enough, Bryn. This fight is mine."

Brynjolf chuckled and then coughed in pain.

"You know why I chose the clan of Boar?" Hillevi glared at Adania.

"It's not for their grace, fertility, or strength, I'm sure."

Hillevi snorted. "Gods no, little wolf. This was the clan that killed your beloved daddy. I thought they would be able to end the wolf and dragon line, but it seems that I have to do it myself."

Gods, this woman is unhinged, all because Brynjolf didn't want to bed her?

Adania felt far more focused than she had ever been before.

Smirking, Adania looked at Hillevi. "You honestly think that's going to distract me?" She was uncharacteristically calm. A seething, burning, violent rage was building within her.

Is this what father meant? She thought to herself. *The rage of Fenrir?*

Moments felt like an eternity, and before she knew it, she was on top of Hillevi. Both of them bloody and Hillevi lay silent.

Adania had never felt anything like that before. *Is this how the Berserkers of Bear clan feel?*

Coming off the adrenaline high, she felt the world start to spin. Crawling off of Hillevi, she puked... Violently.

"Elska? You alright?"

Shit... Bryn...

She managed to clear her vision enough to look up at him.

"I've never seen you fight like that."

"Gods, Bryn..." She scrambled over to him.

"You're still as beautiful as the day I raided Jokolvikra."

"Don't you die on me... I'm not ready for that."

His breathing was shallow, and blood dripped down his face from a missing eye.

"Damn dragon." She managed to help him get up and walked up to the training grounds where the last of the clan was gathering.

Revna and Helga ran over to the two.

Adania and Brynjolf were both covered in blood, and both collapsed on the training grounds dirt.

Adania awoke with a violent headache. Finding herself in a bed in Randvi's hut. Well... Revna and Helga's hut now.

Revna almost dropped what she was holding. "She's awake!" She yelled making Adania groan in pain.

"So loud..." she growled.

"Forgive me, Jarlskona... We thought you weren't going to wake at all."

Adania sat up and what felt like fire rippled through her ribs and into the rest of her body making her want to puke from the searing pain. "Where's Brynjolf?"

"He's in Helga's bed resting. You both took quite the beating. He is breathing and bruised and he's also missing an eye."

Oh... right... Hillevi.

Adania looked up at Revna. "Thank you for taking care of us. How are the kids?"

Revna moved aside to show that Gunnar was sitting in a chair hunched over on a table fast asleep. "He has been going back and forth between you and Brynjolf to make sure that you both are taken care of. He has a way with herbs and medicines... And Helga and I have been taking shifts with Eilif and Runa."

She let out a sigh of relief, "I'm glad they are okay... How long have we been out?" Adania stood up and wobbled slightly.

"The better part of three days. We have been doing your wolf rituals like Randvi had taught us and we were so worried that they wouldn't work..."

Adania chuckled slightly. "Bryn and I are a little too stubborn to die just yet."

Revna snickered then, trying to make sure not to wake Gunnar, despite being the one that yelled to Helga earlier.

"And what of the clan of Boar?" Adania's eyes narrowed slightly.

Revna sighed. "Hillevi is no more, and the Jarl of Boar clan awaits judgment from you and Brynjolf."

"Has Brynjolf woke at all?"

Revna nodded. "He's been in and out. Asking about you or the kids at times, but he's restless when he sleeps. You are the first to stand and move around like you are."

"Then I guess I have a husband to try and wake."

Adania kissed Gunnar on the forehead gently before going to the other room where Brynjolf was.

Curled up against his chest lay a sleeping dark-haired girl.

"Runa…" Adania whispered softly. Pushing hair from her face she kissed her temple before kissing Brynjolf on the forehead.

His good eye looked up at her. "Elska? Are we in Valhalla?" He groaned.

"No, my love… We are still on Midgard, in Jokolvikra."

He smiled up at her and started to sit up. "I guess I'm like Odin now huh?"

"Missing an eye? Yea. Though I don't think it's going to grant you any special wisdom or knowledge." she teased. "Still as handsome as ever though." Adania smiled at him. Picking up Runa, she held her tightly for a little while before handing her back to Brynjolf.

"I think I'm going to stay sitting for a little while longer." He spoke softly and put his hand on Runa's head. "I'll speak with the clan tomorrow on the rebuilding of the longhouse."

"Alright, but you aren't doing it alone. We also have to address the Jarl of Boar… He's apparently still here. Most likely Ulfric has him tied up somewhere."

Chuckling slightly, Brynjolf shifted in the bed. "Most likely… If he hasn't killed him already."

"He better not have," Adania stood with her hands on her hips. "but I'm going to go check on Eilif. You get some rest." With that she kissed him softly and then left the room.

Helga and Revna met her in the hallway, holding the small red-haired boy.

Adania picked him up from Helga's arms. "I'm so happy all of them are safe. I was so worried when I saw the longhouse on fire." She sighed.

Revna nodded. "Your mother instincts took over."

Adania held Eilif and kissed his forehead. "It was terrifying."

Helga put a hand on Adania's shoulder. "It's over with now and let's hope it never happens again."

"Agreed. I'm just not looking forward to talking to Baard." She sighed. "But that will have to take place once Brynjolf is feeling better… I don't want him pushing himself."

Revna nodded again. "You both really need to stay in bed and rest."

After a few more days in bed, Adania and Brynjolf were walking through the village to assess the damage that Baard and Hillevi had wreaked.

Several homes and shops would need to be rebuilt, including the longhouse.

Adania sighed. "What if we made a house for us to live in and we make the longhouse more for a mead and feast hall? Or just use it for gatherings and festivals? Then if it gets set on fire again we don't have to worry about rebuilding the kid's rooms, and that's *if* it should happen again." She looked up at Brynjolf.

"If that is what you think we should do. I will gladly do so if it means that you and the kids will be safer."

She smiled up at him as Eilif reached up toward Brynjolf.

Brynjolf took the boy and held him as the couple continued to walk through the village, making their way to the brewery.

Runa and Gunnar came running up to them. "We checked the other side of the village so that you wouldn't have to." Gunnar grinned.

"You did?" Adania smiled and patted them both on the head. "And what seems to be the damage."

"The aver-ee-ary.." Runa spoke and kicked Gunnar when he laughed. "The birdie place..."

Adania sighed. "Runa, don't kick Gunnar... and Gunnar don't laugh when she's trying to say something. You both are still learning."

Gunnar sighed then and looked at Runa. Runa stuck her tongue out at him and looked back up at Adania and Brynjolf. "As I was speechin'... The birdie place needs to be re-build-ded... The birds are all safe though. That's what Hrafn said anyway..."

Gunnar nodded. "Hrafn said that everyone was safe and accounted for."

"That's what I said." Runa pushed Gunnar over.

"Runa! Behave." Adania scolded.

Runa pouted. "Sorry, mommy."

Adania sighed. "You two need to stop picking on one another."

Gunnar looked up at Adania. "But the fisherman's hut is going to need to be replaced and the stables are basically gone."

Runa nodded. "And the baked place needs fixin' and so does the fabric place."

Brynjolf just snickered as he watched the kids interact with Adania.

A black eye patch of leather hugged his head over his left eye.

"Thank you for letting us know. How about you two go play so that me and daddy can deal with this... Or you can go train."

Runa took Gunnar's hand and pulled him toward the temporary training grounds.

"For the love of Thor, Runa... All you ever want to do is have a sword."

Brynjolf grinned and looked at Adania. "She is much like her mother."

Adania just shrugged. "I think it's the wolf in her... Though I'm sure Eilif will be just like his father."

"Don't curse our child with such things." He teased and kissed her softly then. "We have a Jarl to go speak with..." His eye narrowed slightly.

"Brynjolf... It will be fine." She put a hand on his cheek.

Leaning into her hand, she felt the stubble on his face from the last few days of not having shaved it. "That clan took in a woman who was banished from our own. That is against the laws we have been living by for gods know how long... and on top of that they tried to kill you and my kids... He's lucky I haven't been able to do much because I've been recovering from injuries that that bitch gave me... I can't believe she managed to get me on the ground." He sounded frustrated with himself.

Adania took his hand gently.

He always seemed so critical of himself when it came to battle or training.

"Bryn... She's gone. I'm still here as are all three of the kids. They didn't win. Though with you missing an eye and how badly you were bleeding... I was worried that I was going to lose you..." She sighed. "I still can't believe Hillevi managed to take an eye from you."

"It pisses me off that she did so too."

"Think it will grant you any extra wisdom?" She teased.

He grinned and shook his head. "Elska... you are so bad at jokes."

"It made you smile so it did what it was supposed to... No matter how bad it was."

The couple shared a laugh as they walked the rest of the way around the main thoroughfares and back up to the building where Baard was being kept.

"Addy, do you really want to come with me? You can stay out here with Eilif. I might get severely angry and possibly kill him."

Adania shrugged. "I'm sure it will be fine, but if you wish for me to stay out here with the boy then I will... I might go over to the training grounds and check on the other two and how they are doing in their training."

Brynjolf nodded. "Go do that. I don't want you to see or hear how angry I'm about to get."

Handing Eilif to Adania, he kissed her forehead and waited for her to leave before he walked into the small hut.

What seemed like ages later, Brynjolf came out of the hut. His hands were bloodied as were his clothes. "Addy is going to kill me." He said to himself.

Ulfric came up to him then and whistled. "You'll be lucky that that's all she does to you." He chuckled. "But you are gonna have to change. I don't think she's going to want to hug you when you're covered in blood."

"I'm more concerned about Runa, Gunnar, and Eilif seeing me like this."

"Well, let's get you changed and I can take your filthy ones to Astrid and see if she can get all the blood out."

"Thanks, Ulfric. You're like a brother to me. I'm happy that you've stayed with me all this time."

Ulfric shrugged, much like his Jarl, he didn't show emotion very often, but he gave Brynjolf a hug. "I'll be here for as long as the gods allow me to be."

The two headed to the small house that Brynjolf and Adania had been using while the longhouse and their new home were being built.

Brynjolf quickly cleaned up, then changed before handing the blood-soiled clothes to Ulfric. "And do tell Astrid not to tell Adania about that."

"I can tell her, but that doesn't mean she won't tell your wife... And sorry Brynjolf, but your wife scares me far more than you do." He chuckled.

"Why is that?" Brynjolf cocked an eyebrow at Ulfric.

"Because she's unpredictable, much like her clans name sake. She is also much like Fenrir... She has strength, ferocity, and fearlessness to her... Also much like a wolf, because of that unpredictability... It scares the shit out of me."

Brynjolf laughed, "You make her sound as though she is some terrifying beast of a woman."

"Brynjolf... As your friend, she is your wife and I would never describe her as such a thing. However, as your clansman... She absolutely terrifies me... I love talking to her, helping out, and training. I know you don't see her as a terrifying force. The way you look at her when she speaks about the things she loves and the things she hates. You are absolutely wrapped around her finger and that's perfectly fine."

Brynjolf looked at his long time friend and slapped his hand against his back. "She's also the mother of my children and yes I am in love with her."

Ulfric smiled at him, "It's about time that you admit that openly."

Brynjolf hadn't noticed that before.

Leave it to Ulfric to be the one to point it out.

He hadn't actually said 'I love you' to her out in public. Sure, he called her 'Elska' or 'my love'; he was going to have to change that.

"Now that that is over with and you've had your come to Freyja meeting." Ulfric teased as he slapped Brynjolf's back and took the bloodied clothes to Astrid.

Brynjolf walked to the new training grounds and hugged Adania from behind.

"How'd it go?" Adania leaned against him as he buried his face into the crook of her neck.

Letting out a groan of displeasure, he pulled away from her and leaned against the fence. "About as good as you would expect..."

"That good, huh?" She looked at him and noticed that his clothes were different from before. "And you got blood all over you didn't you?"

"Not as much as you would think." He lied and smiled at her, not wanting her to worry. Looking up at the kids playing rather than training, it set his mind and body at ease.

She sighed. "Alright... Fine, I'll take your word for it... You didn't blood eagle the bastard did you?"

Brynjolf looked at her and chuckled as he shook his head. "Elska, what kind of dragon do you take me for?" He teased.

"Bryn..." She looked at him with scolding eyes.

"Elska, he threatened my family. Dishonored our clan. I did what was needed."

Adania sighed. "Bryn, all I ever want, is the truth, that's all. I love you and will do anything for you. If you want revenge then we will take it together; if you want to cry then I will be there for you. If you get angry then I will share that anger. I will share your good times and bad ones. You get upset with me and we get into an argument then you just go into another room until we both calm down and we sort this shit out."

"Is sex always an option?" He smirked.

"Brynjolf!" She hit his chest playfully. "Good gods... Not with the children around... but yes that is an option."

He gave her a half-cocked grin and then kissed her cheek before hopping over the fence to join the two elder children. "Alright, you two. Show me what you got."

Runa gave a wicked grin before looking at Gunnar as they both stopped running around.

"Oh no... Runa, what-"

"For Valhalla!" Runa yelled cutting off her father's words as she and Gunnar ran toward him.

Tackling him to the dirt, all three of them shared a laugh. "Oh no... Elska, I have been brought down by the dwarfs of Nidavellir."

"You are on your own, my love. I have to protect the children." Adania laughed. "I'm sure a one-eyed jotun can take down a couple of the dwarfs." She teased.

"Elska, you wound me... Here, your husband calls for aid and you tell him no."

"I know my husband can handle himself."

"Alright fine." He sighed, then let out a growl as he picked himself and the two that tackled him up off the ground.

"Told you," Adania smirked. "Now. Let's go get some food and spend some time together as a family."

Brynjolf carried Gunnar and Runa back to the small house that they were calling home.

Gunnar crawled onto his back and Runa wrapped herself around an arm.

Adania carried Eilif and laughed as the three in front of her played and joked and laughed the entire time back to the house.

Epilogue

Industriousness

"If something is worth doing then it is worth doing well."

Jerrick met with Adania and Brynjolf a few days later with more wood. "You two are going to owe me big for this." He teased trying to lighten the mood.

Several of the clansmen would need to have funeral pyres and Randvi would need a tomb in the base of the mountains where the rest of the seers had been laid to rest.

Adania welcomed Jerrick on the shores of Jokolvikra. "I appreciate the humor but not right now Jerrick."

"How's Brynjolf and the kids?" When he had received her cryptic letter to bring more wood for them and he had feared the worst.

"Brynjolf and the kids are fine. Though Brynjolf is missing an eye now, but he's still as ornery as ever."

Jerrick let out a sigh of relief. "Good, I'm glad that your family is alright."

"We have what feels like thousands of pyres to do and a tomb to deal with..."

Jerrick nodded. "I will stay as long as you need and help out where I can."

Adania smiled then. "Thank you, Jerrick. You are more than welcome to stay with Brynjolf and me."

"I might take you up on that… Though I could stay on my long boat if I need to. I don't want to be a burden."

"Nonsense." She walked with him up the hill to the house. "We're going to start on the pyres tomorrow as well as Randvi's tomb. I have a few of the miners going to dig out her spot in the mountains. But Hillevi is gone as is Baard… Though I hope that Nidhogg feasts on Hillevi's rotten corpse."

Jerrick sighed and looked at her. "So… Does that mean that you will merge Boar with Dragon?"

Adania shrugged then. "I'm not sure. I'm sure it is going to be up for discussion with Brynjolf. Though he has been busy with bodies and families while I have been delegated to make sure everything goes the way it's supposed to."

"Well, I'm here and Ivar is here somewhere."

"You didn't leave him to watch over Serpent?"

He shook his head. "No, I have my advisors doing that. This was more important and Ivar wasn't going to take no for an answer if I told him that he wasn't coming with."

"Wolf's mead?"

"That's part of it, but he wanted to help out and figured you would need all the extra hands you could get." He finally looked up to see the damage that had been done and whistled. "Boar really made a giant mess of things."

"Tell me about it. Raven clan left a day or so ago to go rebuild their own home, and the surviving Boar members seem to be asking to join us… It seems that Loki has dropped a lot into my lap of late." She sighed. "But we'll get it done."

"Is that my favorite wolf woman I hear?" Ivar's voice rang out from the longboat making Adania turn to look at him.

"Hello, Ivar. Glad to see you. I'm sure Brynjolf will be happy to see you too."

"Not if he insists on flirting with my wife." Brynjolf's voice came from behind her.

Ivar looked at Brynjolf and raised an eyebrow. "Whoa, you got fucked up."

"You should see what happened to the one that caused the missing eye."

They all shared a laugh. Gods knows she needed a reprieve from all the chaos that had been building.

In the coming days after, Ivar, Jerrick, Brynjolf, Ulfric, and Adania made sure to help with the funeral pyres and Randvi's tomb.

Pyre after pyre had been made. It made Adania feel like it went on for an eternity.

Peace talks with what remained of Boar clan would take place seven days after the last pyre had been lit.

Seven days to mourn the fallen warriors, friends, artisans, and family alike.

Adania stood with Brynjolf as he made a speech for the fallen before he lit the first pyre. Jerrick lighting the one after, and then Ivar lighting the third. The three of them went on like this until the last pyre was lit.

She walked alongside Brynjolf as he lit the pyres. Once the last pyre was lit, she stayed until the morning light to make sure the pyres would stay lit through the night.

Jerrick, Ivar, and Brynjolf all woke periodically to check on her; bringing her water or a blanket to stay warm.

The next morning, she was sluggish and exhausted, but she wanted to make sure that the souls had departed Midgard properly and that they would reach the halls that they were meant to rest in.

"Elska, you should rest." Brynjolf hugged her tightly as he wrapped her in his cloak of thick, dark wool.

"I will rest once everything is done." She yawned as she looked at the sun starting to peek over the horizon.

"Addy, you can't keep on like this. You'll get sick... You're already exhausted."

"I know but there is still so much to do... And we have the kids... and then Randvi's tomb."

"Elska, If I had known you were going to be out here all night I would have carried you to our bed so you could sleep. I could have handled this."

She shook her head. "No, you have other things to attend to. I will be alright. I just need to eat some food and drink some tea. I'll be fine."

Brynjolf sighed. "I know there's no use in arguing with you."

"Then why do you continue to try?" She teased and kissed him softly.

"Because one of these days I hope that you won't be stubborn." He chuckled and looked at her. Brushing the hair from her face, he smiled and kissed her forehead. "Let's get you some food. The pyres are almost out... And you are going to take a nap later on. Jerrick, Ivar, and I can handle the kids. You are going to need some kind of sleep later if you plan on staying up all night again with Randvi's tomb."

Adania shook her head. "No, I'm not going to stay up again. I just wanted to make sure that these made it to their gods' halls on time."

He smiled at her. "Alright Elska, let's get you back home and warmed by the fire."

Getting up, she brushed herself off from the ash and dirt that had collected on her apron dress. "This is gonna have to get washed... several times." She sighed. "But oh well."

Walking back up toward the house, they spoke about the day ahead.

Breakfast, checking on the tomb, lunch, preparing everything for Randvi's funeral, dinner, and then Randvi's funeral.

Putting on her cloak, Adania went to check on the ones that were mining out an alcove for Randvi. She would be laid to rest with the rest of the seers that Wolf clan had buried at the base of the mountain.

Sighing, she walked over to the man that was outside the tomb, "I wanted to check on Randvi's alcove."

He looked at her, "It's practically done. We've been working as fast as we can."

"If we need to hold off for a day or two then we can."

He shook his head, "No need, Jarlskona, It will be done within a few hours."

Adania smiled slightly, "Thank you."

"Not a problem. Just leave it to us. You go and be with Brynjolf and the kids. Relax a little bit. I heard you stayed up all night to make sure the pyres stayed lit... My brother was among the fallen. I appreciate you doing that for us while we all tried to sleep."

"It wasn't a problem. I don't mind doing so if it makes it easier on the families."

"So let us do this and you go take a break for once."

Adania chuckled slightly then, "Alright, fine. Thank you for doing this for Randvi."

"No need to thank me, Jarlskona. Let us handle all that needs to be done here. You go and relax with your family."

"Still, thank you either way," she smiled and turned to leave.

Going back to the house, she went and hugged Brynjolf tightly. "I think I'm going to eat and then I'm going to lay down for a little while… to try and rest like everyone keeps telling me to."

Brynjolf smiled at her and nodded, "Alright Elska. I'm sure I can handle the kids for awhile. Plus if they get to hard to handle then I will just go get Jerrick and Ivar," He looked at her then.

"Thank you, Bryn." She touched his cheek and kissed him gently.

After eating lunch, she went to the bedroom to take a nap and slept for only a couple of hours. As she slept, she dreamt.

Randvi sat at a table with food and drinks. "Wolfling… Come have one last meal with me."

"Randvi… I'm sorry that I couldn't protect you."

The old woman shook her head. "Don't be sorry or worried Jarlskona. I am with Freyja. Gunnar, Runa, and Freyja were the ones that greeted me to the halls of Sessrumnir. They are proud of you and proud of their son."

Adania sat at the table across from Randvi, "I miss them… and you."

Randvi took Adania's hand in hers, "We will meet again dear child. Freyja tells me that your father is proud of the Jarlskona that you have become and he looks in on you and the children from time to time when Odin allows."

Adania smiled at her, "Thank you Randvi."

"I saw that you stayed up late to make sure that the souls departed Midgard properly. I guess you were paying attention to some of my lessons."

Adania chuckled, "I just didn't want the gods mad at me for keeping someone longer than we were supposed to…"

Randvi smiled, "The gods wouldn't be mad at you. Maybe a little frustrated but not mad. You follow the gods the best you can and you honor them like you are supposed to. Though I will say, Loki isn't a fan of you calling him names."

Adania blushed some and then laughed, "Maybe he shouldn't make my life difficult at times."

Randvi smiled as they both began to eat on bread and boar, "It's what he does. He does it in order to teach us lessons that must be learned… But you are doing well. Don't doubt yourself. Your husband will take care of you and your children. You both will get to hold your grandchildren. You have suffered the worst already and you handled it."

"I did what needed to be done. I didn't have a choice in the matter."

Randvi nodded, "but you fought through it and didn't give up. That's what makes you a wolf Adania. You are stubborn and though you are small, you are a mighty force to deal with. That's why you needed Brynjolf and he needed you. You bring out the best in one another and your strengths are his weaknesses. His strengths are your weaknesses. You bring balance to one another and that alone is a force, in and of itself, to deal with."

Adania listened and smiled at the seer, "Thank you Randvi, but why tell me all this?"

"Because you needed to hear it."

They continued joking and laughing for a little while longer before the two got up from the table.

Adania hugged Randvi then, "Until we meet again."

"Until we meet again wolfling."

Adania got up and stretched looking out the window seeing the sun was setting.

Once she freshened up a bit, she went out to see Brynjolf with the kids. He was telling stories of his clan.

Leaning against a door frame with her arms crossed under her chest she watched as he told the story.

Runa and Gunnar listened intently to Brynjolf's retelling of the time that he raided Wolf clan and took Adania as his bride.

Adania chuckled making Brynjolf look up and smiled at her. "I was about to come and get you for dinner."

Runa ran over to Adania, "Is it true mom? Did daddy and you fight and that's how you got-ted married?"

Adania bent down and hugged the girl that looked far more like Brynjolf than Adania, "Well, that's mostly true," She winked.

Runa turned to look back at her father, "I can't believe you beat-ted up mom."

Both adults shared a chuckle.

"Runa, that's how all the women in our family find their husbands."

"Oh." Runa thought for a moment then and went back to sit down.

Gunnar was sitting on the floor with Eilif in his lap.

"We need to deal with Randvi's funeral rites. You can either stay here or go with. It's up to you... Though Eilif is going to have to go with us."

Gunnar handed Eilif to Adania then and smiled up at her, "Randvi is with the other seers in the halls of Freyja, and she is happy."

Adania gave Gunnar a pat on the head and kissed his forehead, "I have no doubt that she is happy where she is."

Gunnar smiled at her, "I think I will stay here and watch over the house while you are gone."

"Don't spoil the cat too much while we're out."

Sigurd let out a lazy meow as he curled up on Adania's chair.

Gunnar laughed and nodded, "I promise. I won't spoil him too much.

Runa fixed her hair and went to her parents, "I'm ready to go."

Adania carried Eilif as they walked toward where Randvi's funeral was going to take place.

Torches were lit and Brynjolf gave another speech. Though he hadn't known the woman as long as Adania had, the speech he gave ended up making Adania cry.

After the speech was given, Brynjolf and several more of the males took Randvi's body into the base of the mountain where her alcove had been dug out.

"Rest well, Randvi," Adania sighed.

Brynjolf and the other males came back out moments later, "you alright, Elska?"

Adania nodded, "I will be. Thank you, Bryn," She smiled up at him and kissed him softly.

The years seemed to just fly by after dealing with Hillevi.

Runa, Gunnar, and Eilif became adults almost too quickly in the perspective of Adania and Brynjolf. Runa was getting married to a man from Bear clan; one of the Berserkers.

Gunnar and Eilif were learning how to be Jarls from both Adania and Brynjolf since Eilif would be taking over the clan once Adania and Brynjolf decided he was ready. Gunnar would be his second in command. Much like his mother had been to Adania.

Things now were peaceful; mostly.

Jerrick would visit with his family after he had gotten married.

Raids on Jokolvikra were almost nonexistent as the years went on.

Eilif, Gunnar, and Runa never stopped their training.

Gunnar took to the ax like his mother, Eilif took to the sword and shield like his parents, and Runa took to the bow.

Then there was Brynjolf and Adania, who had the house all to themselves and lived out their days in Jokolvikra telling stories to their grandchildren of the adventures that they had lived through.

Viking/Norse Terms:

Althing – The parliament of Iceland that first convened in 930. Political assembly.

Asgard – The home of the gods.

Baldur – A god in Norse mythology associated with light, wisdom, and courage, although he is never specifically defined as the god of any of these. He is best known for his dramatic death, which heralds the coming of Ragnarok, the end of the age of the Norse gods and the rebirth of the world.

Blood Eagle – A practice that allegedly found torturers separating the victim's ribs from their spine, pulling their bones and skin outward to form a set of "wings", and removing their lungs from the chest cavity. Some depictions of this are brief while others go into more graphic detail. Though the ritual's appearance in medieval texts, of both Old Norse and Latin, are intended to send a message tied to honor as well as revenge.

Elska – A term of endearment. Beloved, loved, etc.

Fenrir – The great wolf in Norse Mythology who breaks free from his chains at Ragnarok, the twilight of the gods, kills Odin, and is then killed by Odin's son Vidarr. Fenrir is the son of the trickster god Loki and brother of the World Serpent Jormungandr and the jotun Hel.

Flyting – A contest consisting of the exchange of insults between two parties, often conducted in verse.

Folkvangr – It's name means "Field of the People" or "Field of Armies" and it's one of the twelve realms in Asgard, inhabited with the bravest of the dead, as well as its ruler Freya and her daughters Hnoss and Gersemi.

Freyja – Probably the most renowned of the Norse goddesses. She's the sister and female counterpart of Freyr and she was in charge of love, fertility, battle, and death. She rides in a chariot pulled by two large cats.

Freyr – He's the ruler of peace and fertility, rain, and sunshine and the son of the sea god Njord. He's also the main fertility god used in Norse mythology.

Gothi – Pagan priest

Hand-fasting – Wedding

Hel – The queen of the afterlife, Helheim. Often referred too as a goddess in Norse mythology, she is half jotun, or giant. Sister to Fenrir and Jormungandr. Daughter of the god Loki and the giant Angrboda.

Helheim – One of the nine worlds of Norse mythology. It is ruled by Hel, the monstrous daughter of the trickster god Loki and his wife Angrboda. This cold, dark and misty abode of the dead is located in the world of Niflheim, on the lowest level of the Norse universe. Helheim is viewed as situated in or on top of Niflheim in stories.

Hersir – a local Viking military commander.

Holmgang – A duel practiced by early medieval Scandinavians. It was a legally recognized way to settle disputes. Typically held on an island. The total ***fighting*** area was no more than about twelve feet ***square***

Jarl – A title given to the highest noblemen in ***Norse*** times

Jarlskona – feminine version of Jarl

Jormungandr – Known as the Midgard Serpent, or World Serpent, in Norse mythology who encircles the realm of Midgard. He is the son of the god Loki and the giantess Angrboda. And also brother of the great wolf Fenrir and Hel, Queen of the Dead.

Jotun – The giants in Norse mythology. Live in Jotunheim

Kransen – Nordic definition roughly translates to "head wreath". It's an accessory worn by unmarried girls and passed down from mother to daughter. Typically this head piece would last for several generations.

Loki – The wily trickster god of Norse mythology, also the father of Hel (Goddess of the underworld), Jormungandr (The great serpent, and Fenrir (The wolf who bites off one of the hands of Tyr and who kills Odin during Ragnarok.

Midgard – The home of man. Earth.

Nastrond – One of the sections of Helheim. Also known as "the shore of corpses". There stood a castle facing north; it was filled with the venom of serpents, in which murderers, adulterers, and perjurers suffered torment, while the dragon Nidhogg sucked the blood from their bodies.

Nidhogg – A dragon who gnaws at a root of the world tree, Yggdrasil. The monster also figures in the punishment of criminals. He rules over the dark shores of corpses, to which the corpses of murderers, adulterers, and oath-breakers are banished. A terrifying hall, with walls woven from serpents and a ceiling that drips venom, waits for these criminals, and inside the hall, the dragon chews on their bodies.

Nidavellir – The realm of the dwarfs. Is also associated with the dark elves in some texts.

Niflheim – The far northern region of icy fogs and mists, darkness and cold. It is situated on the lowest level of the universe. The realm of death, Helheim is part of the vast, cold region. Niflheim lies underneath the third root of Yggdrasil, close to the spring Hvergelmir.

Norn – Goddesses of fate and destiny of both gods and men. The Norn are said to visit each newly born child to allot his or her future.

Odin- Described as an immensely wise, one-eyed old man, Odin has by far the most varied characteristics of any of the gods and is not only the deity to call upon when war was being prepared but is also the god of poetry, of the dead, of runes, and of magic. He has two sons, Balder by his first wife Frigg and Thor by Jord. Odin also has several animals: two ravens known as Hugin and Munin (Thought and Memory) that fly around the world and report back what they see. Sleipnir, the eight-legged horse, can run through all the nine worlds, and then there's Geri and Freki who are Odin's wolves.

Skal – "Cheers"

Skald – A poet. These men held the entire ***Viking*** culture in their heads.

Skuld – means "Debt" or "Future". One of the Norn.

Thor – Norse god of thunder, the sky, and agriculture. He is the son of Odin. Thor is the defender of Asgard, realm of the gods, and Midgard, the human realm.

Thrall – Old Norse term for a slave that could earn their freedom through working. Vikings acquired slaves primarily on their expeditions to Eastern Europe and the British Isles. They could also obtain Viking slaves at home, as crimes like murder and thievery were punished with slavery.

Urdr – means "Fate". One of the Norn.

Valhalla – The hall of slain warriors, who live there blissfully under the leadership of the god, Odin. Valhalla is depicted as a splendid palace, roofed with shields, where the warriors feast on the flesh of a boar slaughtered daily and made whole again each evening. They drink liquor that flows from the udders of a goat, and their sport is to fight one another every day.

Verdandi – means "Happening" or "Present". One of the Norn.

Yggdrasil – an immense and central sacred tree. Around it exists all else, including the Nine Worlds.

CPSIA information can be obtained
at www.ICGtesting.com
Printed in the USA
LVHW112101191222
735554LV00004B/112

9 781637 679067